PENNY CORNER ROAD

A COLLECTION OF SHORT STORIES

PHILIP M. MATHIS

ISBN-13: 978-1-937937-16-4

First Edition

Printed in The United States of America

Twin Oaks Press
twinoakspress@gmail.com
www.twinoakspress.com

Design
Art Growden

*To all who contributed
to the making of these stories*

Preface

Penny Corner Road is a collection of stories inspired mainly by my early life on Penny Corner Road, an actual place in northern Graves County, Kentucky. Exceptions include *The Bird Man*, *Mountain Dancer*, and *Lesson Learned* which are based on post-boyhood experiences. *Hannah's Quilt* is also an exception as it relates more to my mother's life than to my own. Names of actual people and places are frequently used, and in most cases the events described really transpired. Nevertheless, at least some element of fiction remains in every story.

Penny Corner Road was written to entertain and amuse, but I hope it will ultimately prove to have greater worth in that the stories conjure images of earlier times and a now-dying way of life. If these stories awaken sleeping memories or provide glimpses of what life was like for a boy growing up in rural Kentucky during the 1950s, an important goal will have been achieved.

– PMM

TABLE OF CONTENTS

Spring Plowing

Far upstream in the headwaters of my memory, I can see him. He is standing by the barn door holding a pail of warm milk, savoring the freshness of a new day. The pre-dawn light and the mist of early morning impart a subtle softness to the barnyard scene. The air is spiced with scents of baled lespedeza and crushed corn mixed with black-strap molasses. Contentedly he stands, musing on the activities of the approaching day, seemingly oblivious to the footfall of hoofed animals and the muted clucks of gallinaceous birds disturbed, but not alarmed, by the daily milking ritual.

When the sun slips above the horizon an hour later, he is busy in the branch bottom north of the barn, following a horse-drawn plow. As the morning wears on, the angle of the sun changes so the rays are more direct. Soon his blue chambray shirt is soaked with sweat causing it to cling as if magnetized to his muscular body. The day is still young. As yet the plowman shows no signs of fatigue. The sweat cools and soothes his muscles forestalling the weariness that is sure to come. His workday is long, twelve hours of following the plow, lifting and swinging it to start each new furrow and admonishing the sometimes-onerous horses. The day is not without its rewards, though: the sound of the disk-like coulter slicing the soil, the sight of red-wing blackbirds and meadowlarks foraging along the deep furrows, scents of winter-mellowed earth, and the sounds of leather harness against perspiring horseflesh.

The work is muscle numbing, but he is a man equal to the task before him. His physique is highlighted by an especially impressive upper torso. His chest and shoulders are big and strong, almost as powerful as those of the draft animals he commands. The squareness of his shoulders is tempered by rounded deltoids and bulging biceps. At twenty-eight, he is in the prime of life. Neighbors have often commented that he could "drive any team of horses in the county until they dropped in their traces."

It is after sundown when he returns to the barn. As he unhitches the horses in the deepening twilight, the tinkling of chains and the faint groans of leather moving against leather can be heard. In the direction of the sounds, neither man nor beast is clearly visible, but the weariness of each can be sensed. At last he completes the unharnessing, collars and wooden hames are hung on their pegs, and the day's work comes to a close. The horses are released from their shackles and are suddenly free to snort and wallow on their backs in the dust outside the barn.

A dimly lit kitchen window serves as a beacon as the plowman slowly winds his way toward the house in gathering darkness. Inside he finds companionship and a meal of salt-cured bacon, creamed corn, mashed potatoes, and spring lettuce. For a second course, he eats hot biscuits, butter, and sorghum molasses. The supper conversation concerns the progress of his work and prospects for the spring planting. His wife—my mother—listens carefully and comments only occasionally as he outlines his plans.

After completing my nightly chore of filling the wood box behind the Rome Eagle cookstove, I venture outside where I find him lying on his back in the grass beyond the porch. He is gazing up at the stars of early evening with hands clasped behind his head. The gentle stirring of the now-cool air serves as a tonic to his overworked muscles.

Although I am only a child, I can sense that his work is hard and his responsibilities are great. He needs my comforting. As I approach him, I see that the evening air has relaxed him and he is at peace with the world. He shows only faint awareness as I lie down to nestle my small body against his massive frame. Without a word, he extends his arm to provide the perfect pillow for my head. The rise and fall of his chest, the warmth of his body, and the chill of night combine in pleasant counterpoint to give me an unequaled sense of security. Alongside him I feel safe. I know that he is powerful, that his strength can conquer the land. He is an able provider. There is nothing to fear, no cause for worry. He is my protector, my hero, my daddy.

Trading at VeuCasovic's

During the 1950s, life in rural western Kentucky was an everyday struggle. At least it was for me and my family. In the spring of '51, a memorable event occurred during a routine visit to VeuCasovic's Store in Lowes. I was almost nine years old, and my brother Steve had turned three a few months before. We didn't get the chance to travel much, and a trip to Lowes always offered the prospect of excitement, a welcome deviation from the daily humdrum.

Our neighbors were mostly small-scale farmers who managed to make a living by growing tobacco patches and big vegetable gardens. Tobacco was a cash crop, one that could be sold for good money, but tobacco growing required almost year-round attention and a good deal of hard work: building plant beds, planting, hoeing, cultivating, suckering, worming, topping, cutting, hanging—and for the dark, fire-cured variety, smoking with low-heat sawdust fires. That was not all. When the cured leaves achieved just the right amount of moisture, there was a process, or stage, called "coming into case." There was also stripping, tying the leaves into bundles called hands, bulking, and preparing baskets for market. By the time a crop was sold in December or January, it was almost time to burn a new plant bed. Afterwards, the cycle would begin again: new seeds would be sown, a coverlet of gauzy fabric would be stretched over the bed to create a kind of hot house. The wait for new seedlings, or sets, to grow would finally end, and it would be time to plant, hoe, and cultivate again. During the brief winter lull, a farmer might find time to rive new tobacco sticks from straight-grained hickory or oak. There was always something to think of, something to do; tobacco was a crop for the industrious, not for the lazy or faint of heart.

My father gave up cigarettes and tobacco farming shortly after he heard the Gospel and joined a religious sect that frowned on everything to do with tobacco. Although the *Bible* makes no mention of tobacco per se and seldom references weeds, tobacco was forsworn because it was a weed, at least by some people's definition. The fact that we didn't grow tobacco meant we had to compensate for the lack of income in other ways. We did this mainly by having a larger-than-usual flock of egg-laying chickens, raising hogs and calves for sale, selling hay and corn, and milking three or four Jersey cows. From the chickens and cows, we produced eggs and cream for sale or trade at Junior VeuCasovic's General Store in Lowes, a crossroads town whose population might have been around a hundred.

Steve and I always begged to ride along when Daddy went to Lowes to sell or trade our farm goods for things we needed: meal, sugar, flour, salt, oatmeal, etc. Our only means of conveyance over the rutty, gravel roads that led to Lowes was a 1947 Willys-Overland Jeep. Given the day-to-day isolation we experienced, the three-mile ride to Lowes never failed to spur a sense of adventure. It represented an opportunity to see new things, meet new people, and possibly get a candy bar and a Pepsi.

As a family, we welcomed visitors and always enjoyed visits with relatives and neighbors, but outside the environs of our farm and home, we tended to be shy, a bit uncertain. Some might even say backward. This was true for my parents as well as for Steve and me. One Saturday in what may have been the month of March, we—Daddy, Steve, and I—set out toward Lowes with a few dozen eggs and a stainless steel bucket full of cream. Our mission was simple. We would trade the eggs and cream for food staples or other items Mama needed around the house. The ride past Otey Ross', Clarence Voyles', Mr. Emmit Sanderson's, and Eldon Puckett's was a treat, but when we got to VeuCasovic's Store, the excitement really began.

Steve and I followed Daddy into the dimly lit store, our eyes sweeping about in wonder. To the left was a shed annex with bags of feed for livestock. Toward one end was the office of Dr. Lloyd Simpson, the doctor who delivered Steve and me. At the back, in the main part of the store, galvanized tubs hung on the wall above a bench stocked with hardware and other things: nails, screws, hammers, buckets of paint, paint brushes, pry bars, small wrenches, bridles and other harnesses, log chains, and so on. At the front was a counter with a big wood-and-brass cash register, a pickle jar, and several jars stocked with hard candy. Also, there were chocolate bars, peanuts, and other snacks. Toward the rear of the store, along the north side, sat a top-loaded ice box containing a mix of cold drinks: Pepsi, Coke, NuGrape, Royal Crown Cola, Double Cola, Orange Crush, Seven-

Up, and Dr. Pepper. Corn meal, flour, syrup, salt, black pepper, baking soda, sugar, fresh light bread, soda crackers, and many other edibles were displayed on tiered shelves down the middle of the store. Young folks like Steve and me could hardly take it all in. In fact, I had not noticed anyone in the store except the proprietor, Junior VeuCasovic, until we were about ready to leave. By then, our goods had been sacked up, ready for departure. Daddy lingered to drink his Pepsi and eat a Three Musketeers bar. Steve and I enjoyed snacks as well.

Daddy knew many of the people in Lowes. He knew Junior VeuCasovic had a three- or four-year-old nephew named Steve. In fact, he had noticed him darting about the store shortly after we arrived, but my brother and I had not noticed him and did not really know him even though we may have laid eyes on him on some prior occasion.

Seeing my brother eyeing the storekeeper's nephew, Daddy asked, "Why don't you go over and ask that little boy what his name is?"

My brother looked uncertain but after a moment's hesitation did as he was told, asking, "What's your name?"

The boy boldly responded, "Steve. What's yours?"

My brother suddenly looked flabbergasted, paused a second, and finally murmured: "I don't know. You've got me all mixed up now!"

No doubt my brother has grown tired of the story being retold over the years and decades since, but Daddy and I enjoyed a good laugh that day—the day my brother forgot his name.

The Christmas Gift

During my boyhood, there was a span of time when a large group of uncles, aunts, and cousins gathered at my maternal grandmother's house to celebrate special occasions. The first of these gatherings I recall began one cold, gray Christmas morning. Our Model B Ford wouldn't start, so my father hitched our horses to the only other means of conveyance we had—an old, iron-tired International wagon. I snuggled between my parents on the wide board that spanned the wagon bed near the front. It was not a comfortable way to travel, but we were unaware of our deprivation as we set out over the two miles of unpaved roads that led to Grandmother's house.

I liked traveling the dirt, farm roads along Brush Creek Bottom and alongside Owen's Chapel Graveyard but hated the noisy and bumpy gravel-covered stretches. The grinding of the wagon's iron tires against the brown gravel created a near-deafening cacophony, forcing my parents to speak in loud voices. Even then, entire phrases were sometimes lost in the rasping, grating, scratching, and screeching of iron against rock. I entertained myself by humming in a low monotone and listening to the random wavering of my voice as the wagon jolted along.

What made the journey pleasant, though, were the stretches of dirt road. Here it was calm and peaceful. The tinkle of the trace chains, the muted murmur of leather harness, and the rhythmic footfall of horses intermingled pleasantly. I loved these parts of the journey. The contrast of the warmth of my parents' bodies and the nip of the winter air against my face felt good. I liked the clouds of moisture that sprang from the nostrils of the horses. I liked the musty smell of leaf decomposition in the wooded areas along the creek road and the naked, white trunks of sycamores set against the drab landscape. But more than anything, I enjoyed boyish fantasies of tawny-skinned Shawnee braves lurking along the trail, hiding in the undergrowth, moving stealthily among the trees. As the wagon rolled along, I imagined glimpses of feather-fletched arrows, pipe tomahawks, skinning knives, and other Indian-style weapons.

For a youngster, time passes slowly. The journey seemed endless, but at last we were there. My father tended the horses while Mother and I made our way to the front porch. She carried pecan pies she had baked, and I carried three small packages wrapped in paper saved from past Christmases. On the porch, we were greeted by my grandmother and two of Mother's unmarried sisters. Having no children of their own, these aunts doted on me and other nephews and nieces. The greeting was a mixed blessing. I enjoyed the attention and hugs but dreaded the kisses, especially those from my aunts. Even when I turned to the side, they always managed to plant a big, moist kiss squarely on my mouth. Grandmother's kiss wasn't too bad. It was always delivered with dry, pursed lips, and I didn't have to wipe my mouth afterwards. Her gentle hug and pat on the head actually made me feel good.

As we were ushered in from the outside, relatives converged on us from all directions. Their talking, laughing, and gesturing created a noisy hubbub that made us feel welcome. After Granddaddy took our coats and wraps, we stood in front of the fireplace enjoying its warmth and the mingled sounds of many conversations. The fire was wonderful. Long, yellow-orange tongues rolled upward over big, oak logs, licking the soot-blackened throat of the fireplace.

My near-numb hands and feet soon warmed, and the darkness that had engulfed us as we entered the room gradually gave way to dim light. Through the shuffling crowd, I caught a glimpse of Grandmother's tree. To me, it was an awesome sight: a symmetric red cedar, nearly seven-feet tall, draped all around with strings of popcorn, tinsel icicles, home-made ornaments, and a few delicate store-bought glass balls. At the top was a five-point gold star. Beneath the tree was a billowy bed of home-grown cotton, nearly hidden by a mound of presents. Unconsciously I moved toward the tree, barely able to contain my excitement.

The tree symbolized all that Christmas at Grandmother's included: outdoor play with cousins, a festive meal, and the exchange of presents. Play began shortly after most of the relatives arrived. Weather conditions and other factors dictated the kinds of activities we engaged in, which generally included such things as skating on the frozen pond, exploring Granddaddy's barn, snowball fights, games of tag, hide-and-seek, follow-the-leader, and Red Rover. The meal typically consisted of baked country ham with Grandmother's secret sorghum-molasses glaze, assorted vegetables, casseroles, relishes, and salads. There would also be desserts galore: pecan, pumpkin, and chocolate pie and two or three kinds of cake. The men and older boys always ate first, followed in turn by the women and younger children.

After everyone had eaten, the presents under the tree would be opened. As I thought about the prospect, I began to tingle in anticipation. The mystery and drama had been building for weeks. Names had been drawn in early November, and all except a few had kept the identity of the person whose name they had drawn cloaked in secrecy. Name drawing was invariably accompanied by intrigue, a factor that contributed to the excitement of the season. First, there was the excitement of actually drawing a name. Next, there was the satisfaction of keeping it secret from all but a trusted few. There was also the excitement of shopping for just the right gift. Then there was the delightful uncertainty of not knowing who had drawn your own name and the challenge of trying to guess whom it might be. Last but not least, there was the titillating uncertainty that surrounded not knowing the sort of gift one might receive come Christmas Day. Mischief-making adults sometimes further heightened expectations through remarks intended to mislead nosy listeners.

As I stood there in front of the tree, my hope of getting a pocketknife soared. I knew I was old enough to be trusted with one, and I had made my desire known to my parents and to several relatives. The knife I wanted was not just any knife. I wanted a bone-handled,

Barlow jackknife. I could see it in my mind's eye. It would have brass linings between the backsprings, tiny brass pins through the smooth bone handles, and the word *Barlow* stamped on the prominent metal knuckles. I could imagine its various uses, its feel in my hand, and the dull snap of its blades being closed. I could picture myself whittling idly or paring an apple during lunch at school. Finally, I could imagine the respect I would gain from schoolmates and how they would all want to examine and fondle it. My hopes soared as I recalled how I had interrupted a conversation between my mother and Uncle Ed one afternoon in early December. My unexpected intrusion had resulted in an awkward pause, but just before I had entered the room, I had clearly heard Mama say, "He likes pocketknives, I think." Since that incident I had been fairly certain Uncle Ed had drawn my name. I was encouraged because I was confident Uncle Ed would have a better-than-average notion of the kind of knife a boy would want, and he wouldn't be too Scrooge-like to buy a bone-handled Barlow.

Only with great discomfort did I occasionally allow doubts to enter my mind. Surely anyone would know I wouldn't want something like new socks, a belt, or a crew-neck shirt! And surely anyone who drew my name would remember I had gotten a sack of cat-eye marbles last year and a deluxe box of Crayolas the year before that. If the knife were to be something other than a Barlow, maybe it would be a nice pen knife with a bail at one end so it could be attached to a chain. That wouldn't be too bad, although it certainly wouldn't be a Barlow.

I was about to begin looking for my gift when I was interrupted by two cousins tugging on my sleeve, urging me to put on my coat and come outside to play. I eagerly joined them and was soon engrossed in play. First, we played hide-and-seek in Granddaddy's barn and other outbuildings. After a short session of follow-the-leader, we engaged in a spirited round of cowboys and Indians along the edge of the woods beyond my grandparents' pond. We were just beginning to enjoy taunting a belligerent young bull in a nearby field when we were called to dinner.

During and after dinner, a number of comments were made about how good the food was, but I hardly ate. All I could think about was the Barlow knife. I imagined how I would remove the wrapping, being careful to save the paper for use in the future. I knew Uncle Ed would want to surprise me, and I didn't want to disappoint him. In my mind, I went over and over how I would react. I wouldn't scream with surprise. I would react slowly. Perhaps I would feign being at a loss for words before allowing a big grin to spread over my face. I would thank Uncle Ed politely and then engross myself in examining the knife's features. Later I would repeat my thanks and say how much I liked it and that it was *exactly* what I had wanted.

It seemed like forever before Granddaddy finally assembled the entire group in the living room. Everyone crowded into a big circle: Uncle Ed and Aunt Effie, Uncle George and Aunt Bonnie, Uncle Josh and Aunt Susie, Uncle Andrew and Aunt Hilda. Then there were my mother's sisters, my great-uncle on Granddaddy's side of the family, and more than a dozen of us children. All chairs were occupied, and a few adults had to stand. Children sat on the floor or in the laps of parents.

Granddaddy announced that everyone had been blessed during

the year and that no member of the family had suffered any sort of serious illness. He mentioned how lucky he felt to have such caring children and grandchildren and how his prayers had been answered. He went on to mention that the Lord was the "giver of all gifts" and that we should remember Him as such, especially during Christmas. He talked on and on. Although I knew Granddaddy meant well, all I could think of was how he was delaying the gift opening. The gifts he spoke of seemed either too obvious or too abstract to worry about. The only gift I was interested in was the one Uncle Ed had gotten for me.

At last, Granddaddy finished his heartfelt oration and began to hand out the presents. Aunt Bonnie got the first gift. I knew what it was before she opened it. It was a few yards of calico and a store-bought dress pattern Grandmother had purchased on behalf of Granddaddy. I had overheard Grandmother discussing it with my mother a while back. Aunt Bonnie appeared to be pleased and laughingly teased Granddaddy about how he had done so well in remembering her dress size and favorite color.

My twelve-year-old cousin Wilda was next. She got a book from my mother. As far as I could tell, she liked it, and Mother smiled proudly when she thanked her. Several more gifts were parceled out before Granddaddy held up a small one that looked promising. He announced that it was for a cousin about my age, David. I waited apprehensively for David to open it and was relieved when it turned out to be a pen-and-pencil set from Uncle George.

Granddaddy continued to pass out presents. Soon the room was filled with the sounds of rattling paper and excited voices. Over the din, I heard Granddaddy call the name of my cousin Samuel. The present he held was small, and again my interest and concern grew. I watched with bated breath as Samuel removed the paper revealing a small box. He opened the box and removed a pearl-handled pen knife attached to a delicately woven chain. His face lit up as he announced that it was from Uncle Ed.

I went numb. My suppositions had been entirely wrong. Why had I assumed the knife Uncle Ed and Mother had spoken of was for me? How stupid of me! My Christmas was ruined. I didn't care now. Events became a blur of bitter disappointment. Finally, I overcame the shock enough to realize someone had placed a gift in my lap. I heard my mother say, "Son, aren't you going to open your present?" I looked down, still in disbelief. It looked nice enough, wrapped in what I could tell was brand new paper and tied with a fancy bow. But its size and shape gave away its contents: shoes of some sort, probably house slippers. Before Mother could stop me, I carelessly tore the paper away. It was shoes, all right. The label on the end said Buster Brown. Cousin Sam offered the use of his new pen knife to cut the tape that held the lid on. I ignored him as I hurriedly tried to tear the tape with my fingernail. Having no success, I finally gave in and let Sam slit it with his knife. Inside, the box was stuffed with tissue paper, but there were no shoes. What a cruel joke, I thought. But at that very moment, I felt the outlines of a small box buried within the mass of paper. I tore away the paper, opened the box, and there it was, a bone-handled Barlow. I forgot all about my planned reaction and let out a yelp of unbridled excitement! My prayers had been answered.

Underneath the knife, inside the box, was a neatly printed card, "To a special nephew, Philip." It was signed by Aunt Effie. My emotions took over. I flew straight across the room and hugged her. Later I realized that I had been so busy thinking of what a sweetie she was to have Uncle Ed talk to my mother that I forgot all about her mischief in placing the knife in a shoebox, of all things!

We barely had time to compare presents before my father announced it was time to leave. Sam had complimented my knife and offered to trade, but I declined. I couldn't believe it. I now owned a Barlow jackknife, a knife I later learned had been named for the eighteenth-century European knifemaker Russell Barlow.

The trip home went much faster than the trip to Grandmother's earlier in the day. When I got home, I could not remember passing over smooth dirt roads or rough, gravelly roads. I could not remember passing through Brush Creek Bottom. I could not remember anything that had been said or any fantasies about Indians. All I had thought about was the Barlow knife.

Philip M. Mathis

Schoolyard Scuffles

I wouldn't say I was much of a fighter, but there was a time when I got into a scrap or two. I suppose my fighting started with little-boy tussles with Daddy before I reached school age. Maybe those bouts were too friendly to count since there was never any threat or danger. Daddy would certainly never hurt me. So in looking back, my earliest tussles did little to prepare me for later fights. Useful fighting skills can be learned through acting and simulation, to some degree, but experience is the best teacher.

The earliest skirmish I recall came one Saturday when I was four. Mama was keeping my cousin Ralph while his mother went into town on business. Despite the fact that he was a year younger, Ralph was about my size. The skirmish began with each of us having a toy car that we pretended to drive through the air, making buzzing sounds. During a stop in the action, I asked Ralph to exchange cars with me, thinking he wouldn't mind. After all, both cars were really mine. To my surprise, he steadfastly refused to exchange. Annoyed, I walked over to him, grabbed his car, and began pulling. A tug-of-war ensued during which we each tugged with one hand and hit at the other's arms with the other hand. Not being able to retrieve my car, I appealed to Mama, saying, "Make him give me my car. He's just three, and I'm four!" Mama reconciled our conflict somehow. I'm still not sure whether the fight was a loss or a draw for me, but it sure wasn't a win.

When I entered first grade, I was well behaved and not prone to fighting or bullying on the playground. Still, kids will be kids, and I must admit I eventually discovered I could get the best of most of the boys in my class. One exception was Anthony Crosswright. I might have been able to out wrestle Anthony, but he had been retained in first grade due to insufficient academic progress and was therefore older and bigger than most first graders.

Our bus usually arrived at school half an hour or so before the teacher rang the school day into session. During this time, my older cousins, fifth and sixth graders, "arranged" for me to wrestle Douglas "Mudpie" Turner. Mudpie was the second child of one of the poorest families in our neighborhood. The rumor was that the family practically lived off milk gravy, biscuits, and pork fat. Mudpie's hair was a shade of blond that bordered on white, and his skin was pale, too. Years later, I wondered if he possibly suffered from a protein deficiency of some sort. Perhaps he had a tyrosine deficiency, and his body could not make melanin, I hypothesized. Whatever the nutritional problem, the thing that set Mudpie apart was the green, partially congealed snot that always oozed just beneath his nose.

Mudpie was not averse to wrestling, and I wasn't, either. But neither of us ever picked a fight. My cousins instigated our tussles for their own entertainment. Judging by the regularity of our bouts, fights with Mudpie were a hit. I could usually get on top of him and pin his arms to the ground. During the grappling to get him on the ground, I sometimes felt the coolness of his cheek against mine, something I actually found to be pleasant. Avoiding his nose was the problem; that could be unpleasant. Poor Mudpie; even when he managed to get me on the ground, my cousins intervened by putting me back on top or by restarting the fight. It wasn't fair, I admit, but it gave me experience.

As I progressed through the elementary grades, many of my classmates grew faster than I did. As a consequence, I soon became an average-size boy with a mediocre record as a scuffler. By the time I reached fifth or sixth grade, at least half the boys could out wrestle me. Understandably, I fought less and less and sought to avoid conflict more and more.

Like it or not, it wasn't always possible to avoid fighting. When I reached high school, we took physical education as an everyday subject. The basketball coach taught the boys' classes and always reserved several days for boxing. He issued well-padded gloves—12 ounces, I think—in order to reduce the chances for a concussion, cut, or some other serious injury. My problem with boxing had to do with the way Coach Mason matched up contestants. His method was to pair boys of about the same height with little or no regard for weight, build, or muscle development. I was relatively tall but small-boned and slim, not the best sort of physique for boxing and especially not the best given the coach's criterion for matchmaking.

Although I was a sinewy, lean-muscled farm boy, I suffered more than one lopsided loss during our physical-education bouts. I never got a bloody nose, but I did get a puffed-up face and a busted lip or two. Despite my personal dislike for boxing, I always enjoyed watching classmates box. One year—I think it may have been my junior year—a boy named Jimmie Rovencamp transferred into our school from somewhere in Michigan. Word soon spread that Rovencamp was a boxer, one who had boxed in the Golden Gloves competition while he lived up North.

Palmer Davidson was the best boxer in our class and had been the best for years. He was muscular, compactly built, and had a devastating right hook. No one wanted to box Palmer until Jimmie Rovencamp came around. Rovencamp was a bit too cocky for us, and we were skeptical of his boxing claims. Therefore, we couldn't wait for him to be matched up with Palmer. Palmer was the undisputed alpha male in our class and a boxer like none we'd ever seen. With the urging of a number of boys, Coach Mason agreed to let Palmer go a round or two with Rovencamp one day during the lunch hour. Once the bout began, we were all stunned. Even though Palmer was stout and could deliver a powerful punch, Rovencamp was undeniably quicker, had better footwork, and could deliver punches in barrages. His left-handedness and superior skill soon frustrated Palmer, and Coach stopped the bout. I never forgot that bout and was not surprised to see Rovencamp's name on the undercard of a professional bout a few years later.

Supervised fighting for sport was one thing. No-holds-barred, alley fighting was something else. Such fights occasionally broke out at school. Usually the fight would be between two boys who had developed a dislike for one another over time and who had a history of settling arguments through less-than-diplomatic means. A number of times, I'd stood in the ring of onlookers that defined the arena for combat. I'd watched foes go at it, usually with partisan interest, and I'd been repulsed by the violence that left one or both combatants bleeding and bruised. Even though I was not above being a spectator, I purposed in my heart that I would never enter such a ring.

The events that led up to the day I entered the ring remain fuzzy in my mind. For some reason Billy Joe Ruben hated me. As best I can surmise, his dislike for me had its beginnings in the lunchroom. Billy Joe was slightly ahead of me in the cafeteria line and had just gotten his meal arranged on his tray. As he moved away from the line, one of my so-called friends jostled me, and I somehow bumped Billy Joe, causing him to spill his meat loaf, peas, mashed potatoes, and milk all over the place. The commotion led to a robust round of applause and wolf whistles from the already-seated diners. Billy Joe flailed his messy hands toward the floor, brushed at his soiled clothes, and angrily attempted to get a big dollop of mashed potatoes off his shirt. He looked at me and said, "I'll get you for this, you shithook." I tried to explain I'd been pushed, but he paid no attention.

After that, I tried to avoid Ruben. I'd never actually liked him anyway. He had transferred from a nearby school district and often bragged he had relatives in Memphis. There, he said, he sometimes visited friends and relatives, and he and a few others enjoyed riding around breaking off radio aerials and whacking mailboxes with a lug wrench. He was a thug, I thought, and I didn't like being around him. He seemed to sense my attempts to shun him and scowled at me from a distance a time or two. Once I passed near him with a group of his friends in the hallway. "Hey, fellows! Want to play some squirrel?" he said. I knew what that meant. It meant that he or his friends were planning to grab my nuts and grind them together. I panicked momentarily but was able to veer away and avoid the painful bruising of my testicles.

Not long after that, Billy Joe and his friends caught me outside right after lunch. I was with a couple of friends, talking to a girl just outside the gymnasium. As Billy Joe approached, I noticed he had a bit of mud on his shoe from where it had rained the night before. He knew it, too, because when he got close to where I was standing, he said, "Hey, dipshit, my shoe needs cleaning." His friends chuckled, apparently in awe of Ruben's bravado. I was frozen for a moment but said nothing. I just slinked off toward a low place just off the walkway. Billy Joe pulled away from his friends and took a position on a slight rise about twenty-five feet away and glared at me.

I hoped that my friends would come to my aid or someone would summon the principal or a teacher. Alas, my hope was in vain. My heart sank. Within a minute or two, a circle of onlookers began to form around the two of us. It was surreal. It was like I was a slave at the Colosseum, surrounded by bloodthirsty hecklers. It was not like being an onlooker. Billy Joe continued to insult me. Petrified, I tried to soothe him by asking what I'd done. His only answer was, "You know." The ring of onlookers grew rapidly after someone yelled "fight!" One or two onlookers sang out, "Hey, get it on; don't just stand there." I was still desperately hoping a teacher would arrive to break up the gathering before Billy Joe got hold of me.

My adversary was about my height but heavier, bigger-boned, and more muscular. I was going to get killed, I thought. He was going to beat me like Rovencamp beat Palmer Davidson, except my beating would be with bare fists. I could turn and try to escape the ring, but something wouldn't let me. God help me, I'm going to be disfigured for life!

All of a sudden, it happened. Billy Joe rushed me from his tactical position on the hill. Frozen in disbelief, I remained motionless until he was right on me. I then stepped sharply to my left at a right angle, unintentionally dragging my right leg into the path of Ruben. He tripped on my extended leg and fell flat on his face in the mud! Now I was dead, I was sure. The onlookers were amused. They yelled and derisively pointed at Billy Joe as he got up and began to sling and wipe mud off his face, arms, legs, and the front of his shirt. To my surprise and eternal relief, he parted the ring of onlookers, hopelessly humiliated.

A teacher arrived just as the ring broke up. Billy Joe's friends didn't even try to console him. My friends, however, were elated and congratulated me like a hero. "That was so cool how you tripped Ruben," one said. "You were so quick and in control," another offered. My entourage of friends grew as I walked away, and I could feel my social status rise. "Yeah," I said, "it was funny seeing him sling that mud off his body like mashed potatoes. Maybe we ought to call him 'Mudpie' Ruben."

School Bus Days

When I started school in 1948, my family lived about a quarter of a mile off Shaw Road, a poorly maintained gravel road on the school bus route. Because the bus was almost never on schedule, I had to get to the stop early and wait for twenty to thirty minutes, sometimes in the rain and cold. As I grew older, my parents sanctioned my walking a few hundred extra yards to the closest neighbor's house on the bus route. There I could wait in comfort during inclement weather, but I was admonished not to go there unless the weather was bad.

When I was eleven, my brother Steve started school, at which time Daddy erected a small, privy-like shelter alongside the road. The shelter offered a degree of protection, but the cold and rain still managed to blow in, and it soon became the target of Halloween pranksters who enjoyed tipping it over into the road. More than once, the little building had to be lifted and tilted back into its upright position, but getting it repositioned was always an annoying inconvenience. Finally one Halloween the pranksters moved it into the middle of Shaw Road and burned it. All that was left was the tin roof, a few nails, and a pile of ashes! We never rebuilt it, something I came to regret because cold weather and my use of water as a "styling medium" resulted in ice-crusted, frozen hair on more than one occasion.

Almost everyone who attended school at Lowes got there by bus. In most cases, buses picked up and delivered children along the same route, morning and afternoon, but the bus that served our route actually ran two routes per day. Along one route, pupils were delivered to school about an hour before the school day began. In the afternoon, the same group departed for home without delay. Along a second route, pupils were delivered to school just in time for the school day to begin, but in the afternoon, the pupils on the second route were compelled to wait about an hour while the bus transported children on the other route to their homes. The fact that one bus served two routes ultimately meant that an hour of unsupervised, non-instructional time was added to each school day. This allowed bullying, taunting, and other sorts of social conflict to develop. Squabbles invariably arose as students maneuvered for position in the line to board the afternoon bus. Conflicts typically began with someone allowing a friend or cousin to "cut line" over the protests of students farther back. It was not uncommon for the person authorizing the "cutting" to be whacked on the head with a hardback book. Sometimes both the person authorizing an illegal cut and the person actually cutting line would be whacked, pushed out of line, or slugged on the shoulder.

Riding the school bus itself was even more chaotic. In terms of pure excitement, it easily surpassed events associated with unsupervised before- and after-school waits. Some of the excitement centered on the always-treacherous roads and bridges. But most of the excitement swirled around the personality of our driver, Mr. Henry Barriger, a grumpy, old man we irreverently called "Papa Bear."

My cousin, Ralph Garnett, gave Papa Bear his unwelcome storybook name. "He's always growling about something," Ralph said, noting that calling him Papa Bear seemed to make him growl even more. Papa Bear's face reddened at the slightest provocation, an emotional reaction he often reinforced by clicking the two plates of his false teeth together. We soon learned to annoy him whenever possible. Our job, we thought, was to make his job difficult, hellish, a living nightmare. There were moments when we weren't rowdy or unruly, of course—times when the weather was mild, windows were open, and the smoke from Papa Bear's Lucky Strikes mingled pleasantly with outside air before drifting back into the bus. There were times when the bus ran well and we all enjoyed a smooth, uneventful ride, but those instances were relatively rare. Most of the time, we hurled insults and wisecracks, threw paper wads and small objects at each other or at Papa Bear, yelled or sang too loudly, fought and slapped, slammed one another with hardback books, shot water pistols, smooched and flirted, failed to remain seated, or stood in the aisle while the bus was still moving.

Although Papa Bear was permitted to smoke while driving, the official rule was that students could not smoke on the bus. But the official rule was not always followed. High school boys managed to discreetly smoke in the back of the bus, hiding their lighted cigarettes behind the seat in front of them. They sometimes got away with it but not always. The cigarette itself might be kept out of sight, but wisps of smoke could drift from behind the seat. Papa Bear was good at spotting even a faint wisp of smoke in his rearview mirror. When he saw smoke, the race was on to hide or destroy critical evidence before the Bear could park the bus and make his way down the aisle for an on-the-spot inspection. The penalty for being caught was severe. The offender would be thrown off the bus and left on the side of the road to get home or to school by whatever means possible.

Like many buses of the era, ours was derived from a gasoline-powered, single-axle GMC truck with dual rear wheels and a manual gearbox. Blue Bird, a Georgia company, crafted the body and fitted it onto the truck chassis. A long shifter with a black knob projected from the gearbox just to the driver's right. The transmission gears were not fully synchromeshed, requiring a driver who was adept at double clutching. Mr. Barriger never fully mastered clutching and shifting. Invariably, he ground the gears when he tried to shift to reverse or from neutral into first gear. One could imagine metal shavings being sheared off and falling into the transmission oil. "Grrrr" went the gears, and from the back of the bus, a chorus of voices often rang out: "Put 'er in grandma, Papa Bear!"

The bus could lawfully accommodate up to 54 schoolchildren, though fewer were usually on board. It was new enough to be reliable but nevertheless sometimes balked after being left unattended for a period of time. That was because teenage boys messed around under the hood. A favorite trick was to switch a few wires on the distributor cap, a sure way to frustrate Papa Bear and elicit a call for assistance.

Things came to a head in late November after Papa Bear suffered a series of setbacks. First, heavy fall rains had resulted in the bridge being washed out where Shaw Road passes over Little Brush Creek. This meant Papa Bear's already convoluted route had to be run in a roundabout way with lots of backtracking. It also meant that an almost impossible turnaround had to be negotiated in front of Hector Cullins' place. The angle of the intersection of the Cullins' driveway and the main road was acute, probably around 50 or 60 degrees. It required the driver of a bus such as ours to back up and go forward two or three times in order to negotiate the complete turnaround without backing into a roadside ditch. Papa Bear had difficulty making the turnaround. There was more than the usual amount of gear grinding, accompanied by lots of wisecracking and comments of the "Put 'er in grandma" variety.

Second, Papa Bear had suffered a string of failures in his ongoing attempts to catch teenage boys smoking on the bus. Also, earlier in the week, a front tire had picked up a large nail, causing a flat. This necessitated a long wait while another bus was summoned to rescue passengers who had not yet been delivered to their homes or drop-off points. What hit Papa Bear the hardest, however, was his weekend arrest for hunting Canada geese, or honkers, out of season. It happened in what is known as the Mississippi River Flyway, close to Horseshoe Lake, Illinois. The fine was severe: $200. Even worse was the fact that a number of students on our bus had gotten wind of his arrest and the steep fine.

On the afternoon of the day it happened, Mr. Barriger showed clear signs of stress. It was apparent that he was unusually grumpy and wouldn't suffer smart alecks of any kind. The rockin'-and-rollin' rowdies who rode the bus sensed Papa Bear's mood and were determined to get his goat. As soon as the bus lurched forward, riders conspired to rock the bus by suddenly shifting from side to side in unison. Papa Bear felt the bus sway, scowled into the rearview mirror, and demanded that the movement stop, which it did. But the motion had barely stopped when a small squadron of paper airplanes sailed toward the front of the bus, with the pointed tips of a couple even striking Papa Bear about the head or neck. He demanded that the nonsense stop. Again, his command was heeded.

There was a short lull in action before my cousin, Ralph, a frequent instigator, loudly sang out: "Been doin' any huntin' lately, Papa Bear?" With only this prompt, several wise-offs began to chant "honk, honk" again and again. I almost felt sorry for Papa Bear. To practically everyone's surprise, Papa Bear at first ignored the chants. When the chant continued, though, I could see the red in his face reflected in the rearview mirror, and I could imagine the click, click of his lower plate against his upper.

Suddenly, the bus slowed, and Papa Bear pulled it to the roadside at a point where there was a slight upward incline. He left the engine to idle, kicked the transmission into neutral, and whirled out of his seat, giving the parking brake a passing jerk in the same motion. He rushed toward the back of the bus, determined to put a stop to the "honk, honk" sounds. As he neared the back of the bus, I began to recoil in fear. At about the same time, I noticed the trees outside were creeping past, ever so slowly. Then I realized: No, the trees were not moving. The bus was rolling backwards. In the blur of the moment, Papa Bear also realized what was happening, but it was too late. The bus rolled backwards, across a roadside ditch, then into a good-sized tree before it jolted to a stop!

Papa Bear staggered but remained standing. Confused and apparently unable to remember why he'd come to the back of the bus in the first place, he turned to head back up the aisle toward the front of the bus. As he did, a couple of loudmouthed bullies squawked: "Honk, honk." That was the last straw. Papa Bear turned to confront all of us, his face redder than I'd ever seen it. He opened his mouth wide, as if to shout, but the Poligrip gave way, and his upper plate suddenly came halfway out of his mouth! The bus exploded in uproarious laughter and derision.

The moment was so intense that I can't recall what happened next, but I do remember that no one got hurt and that a small dent remained on the rear emergency-exit door of the bus for a long time.

Roy B.

From a junkyard of old memories, I have salvaged a few recollections of my fifth-grade classmate, Roy B. Smith. Time has blurred the line that once distinguished fact from fiction, leaving me to portray a character of Twainsian proportions based largely on personal recall and unverified rumor. With that caveat, here's what I remember.

Roy B. was the son of a sawmill operator, Roy V. Smith. I don't know exactly where the family lived, but it was somewhere around Boaz or Viola in the northwestern part of Graves County, Kentucky. I don't know where he had gone to school before he came to Lowes, but I do know he had been retained in the same grade level more than once. The reason given for his failure to be promoted was "a lack of academic progress." By the time I knew him, he was a testosterone-saturated fifteen-year-old in a class of still-pubescent eleven-year-olds. He was close to six feet tall, slim but strong, and street wise beyond many adults. His lack of academic progress left him with a disdain for formal education. He often mentioned plans to quit school when he reached sixteen, the age at which attendance became noncompulsory in Kentucky schools.

Roy B.'s self-confidence remained high despite his lack of educational progress. His swashbuckling attitude toward life was apparent to everyone, teachers and classmates alike. The school principal once characterized his behavior as being akin to that of a cocky, young rooster. He strutted and swaggered about, sat with his long legs splayed out in the classroom aisle, and often "acted up" in class. At morning recess and at lunchtime, he frequently led a troop of young disciples, including me, around the schoolyard. As he wandered about, he told dirty jokes and exaggerated stories about his father's sawmill and events in and around the pool hall in Mayfield.

When Roy B. told a dirty joke, he was aware that his young listeners were naïve and that many laughed at the punchline without really "getting" the joke. If someone laughed and Roy B. suspected a lack of comprehension, he would suddenly point his long index finger toward the person who had laughed and say, "OK! You laughed. Tell me what's so funny." If there was any pause, even for a second, he would add with a stare, "You laughed, but you don't know what was funny!" For anyone caught faking an understanding, the humiliation could be almost unbearable. Roy B. could be cruel. Still, he was mostly well liked, and a small flock of us followed him around like sheep after a shepherd.

In good weather, marble games attracted both active players and onlookers during recess and the lunch hour. At Lowes, most marble games were played "for keeps." Playing for keeps meant that a player had to ante—that is, put an agreed-upon number of marbles into the playing ring drawn on the ground with a stick. In return, the player was allowed to keep all of the marbles he shot out of the ring during each game. Playing for keeps contributed, of course, to an unequal distribution of marbles. The better players accumulated huge surpluses that showed up in bulging pockets. Surplus marbles were like wampum; they were a kind of currency. Good players sold them to willing buyers, often the very same individuals who had just lost them! A good player didn't have to sell marbles for money. He could keep them as a sort of trophy or trade them for things like mechanical pencils or pocketknives.

In marbles, Roy B. ran his own racket. He had modified a topless shoebox by cutting a small gap, or door, into the edge of the box. The door was only slightly higher and wider than an ordinary glass marble. When he engaged a willing player, Roy B. would place the shoebox on a level spot on the playground, with the tiny door opening against the ground. He would then pace off a distance of about six feet (two large steps) and mark a line on the ground. He required that a player wager three marbles in exchange for three chances to shoot a marble through the door in the shoebox from the preordained line. Each time a player's shooting marble, or taw, entered the tiny opening, Roy B. would reward the shooter with three marbles. Thus it was possible for a player to win nine marbles by venturing only three.

Roy B., of course, had long ago calibrated the shooting distance and the size of the opening to skew the probabilities in his favor. In fact, most shooters hardly ever hit the tiny door. Roy B.'s shoebox version of the marbles game was so successful that he toted his winnings around in a half-gallon Mason jar. By trading and selling marbles from his jar, Roy B. provided himself with things like cigarettes, bubble gum, and comic books.

There was a designated smoking area behind one of the portable-classoom buildings where smokers gathered during breaks for recess and lunch. Younger students like me sometimes joined the smokers even though we had no cigarettes or reason to be in the area. I guess we somehow felt older or more important by joining the smokers. Roy B. generally smoked his cigarettes down to a short stub. But out of consideration, he would sometimes leave a little extra in order to allow someone else the chance to take a few drags. He'd say, "Hey. You want butts on me?" That was his invitation, and that's how I learned to smoke. I learned a lot of other things from him, too. I learned the p-word, the term SOB, and a lot of bad grammar.

Roy B. often referred to people he didn't like or who annoyed him as being "ignert." He never seemed to be aware of the irony that his mispronunciation of the word implied genuine ignorance. Sometime later, I was reminded that there are actually two kinds of ignorant people: those who don't know but know they don't know and the truly ignorant, those who don't know but don't know they don't know! Even though Roy B. might be truly ignorant by the latter definition, he was not completely ignorant. He knew a lot of things that were not reflected in his school record.

Rumor had it that Roy B.'s school difficulties had begun early at another school. A related rumor suggested his ignorance was at least partly due to his dad's ignorance. According to the story, Roy V. (Roy

B's father) had been in Mayfield one Saturday and by chance met up with Roy B.'s teacher. I think it may have been the year before Roy B. enrolled at Lowes. Anyway, the old man doffed his hat and inquired about how well Roy B. was doing in school. The teacher paused at first but then seized upon the opportunity, "Well, now that you ask, Mr. Smith, I'd have to say that he's not doing very well."

"I hadn't heered that before. What seems to be the problem?" inquired Roy V.

"Well, it's really hard to explain," she said. "He participates in classroom discussions but conveys a sense of reluctance and an attitude that borders on insolence."

"I can lick him and git him straightened out if you'll just tell me what he's doin'," Roy V. replied.

"Mr. Smith, I can't fully explain it. You'd just have to be there to understand."

Hearing her own suggestion spoken aloud, the teacher suddenly hit upon an idea. "Mr. Smith, if you could get to school early some morning without Roy B. knowing and hide in the coat closet, you could listen in and learn exactly what I mean."

"OK," agreed Roy V., and the two arranged for a clandestine visit during the following week.

The agreed-upon date came, and the class began as planned with the old man hiding in the coat closet just inside the classroom. The teacher announced that the topic for study would be "America's Founding Fathers." She then addressed the first question to the troublesome son. "Roy B., tell us who signed the Declaration of Independence."

"I don't know," drawled Roy B. nonchalantly. "I know I didn't."

Hearing Roy B.'s answer, the old man stormed out of his hiding place and yelled, "Gawd dam it, son! If you've signed that dang thing, you're goin' to admit it!" The incident illustrates the sort of ingrained ignorance that followed Roy B. wherever he went.

Another insightful incident was described by the school principal, who reported having encountered Roy B. ambling along the roadside one Saturday evening about dark.

The principal stopped his car and initiated conversation by saying, "Hi, Roy B. I saw some of your friends a little while ago. They were heading for a movie, I think." After a short pause he added, "Why weren't you with them?"

"I didn't have no ride," answered Roy B.

"Well, I've already made three trips up and down this road today. You could have ridden with me."

"Well, if I'da knowed that I coulda rode, I woulda went," Roy B. explained.

Just what had led to the plight of Roy B. and his family was a matter of speculation. Some people recalled the family had once inherited a good bit of money from Roy B.'s great aunt whose estate had included a valuable commercial lot in Paducah. The speculation was reinforced by Roy B.'s occasional allusion to times when things were better for him and his family. He said he could remember how his dad had used the money from his aunt's estate to trade their old truck in on a brand new Oldsmobile—a Rocket 88 with Hydramatic drive. He said the car was great for a while but that they eventually had to use it to haul firewood after giving up the truck. He said his old man had not taken out insurance on the vehicle and they'd been ruined, or "rurined," when Roy V. wrecked it trying to pass a big Packard on a narrow road. By then it didn't matter, Roy B. said. The car was already scratched up, and the passenger seat was a mess from where Roy V. had bled all over it after he cut his hand at the sawmill.

Anyway, by the time I knew him, Roy B. was poor. His attire gave it away. His well-worn dress shoes were laced with cotton twine, and the edges of the soles were attached to the cracked-leather uppers by means of copper rings intended for use in hogs' noses. He wore the same pair of denim jeans again and again. He also wore the same shirt day after day. In winter months, it was a plaid flannel. In warm months, it was a Hadacol T-shirt with the sleeves removed to reveal his shoulders and hairy arm pits.

During fifth grade, our teacher was Miss Rita Pennebaker, an attractive brunette who was madly in love with her husband-to-be, a U.S. Navy corpsman then stationed at San Diego. The girls in the class were interested in the romance and badgered Miss Pennebaker to read her boyfriend's letters to them. Suprisingly, she sometimes did so but always held the letter at an angle in order to deny her listeners the opportunity to discover that she skipped a passage now and then.

Miss Pennebaker smiled a lot and ran her classroom in a manner that older, sterner teachers would not have approved of. She used bribery routinely. She might, for example, promise to read a passage from Mark Twain's *Adventures of Tom Sawyer* just before lunch provided we had not misbehaved earlier in the day. The ploy usually worked, and I loved hearing her read, especially when it came to the passages about Tom and his friend Becky and their getting lost in a riverside cave. The hint of romance always put Roy B. in a special frame of mind.

Before I met Roy B., the word *pussy* only referred to a cat or to some kind of willow tree. It was a word he used often and bandied about in such a way that I knew it could not possibly refer to a cat or a tree! Just what it referred to was not clear, but I surmised that it somehow related to Miss Pennebaker's bare flesh or possibly even her private parts.

While Miss Pennebaker read from *Tom Sawyer* or while she moved up and down the aisles as we filled out pages in our workbooks, Roy B. looked across the aisle at me, gesturing with a gleam in his eye toward Miss Pennebaker. "I wish I could have a piece of that," he whispered. The statement left me puzzled. A piece of what, I wondered. The context of the statement made me realize that it had to do with something good that Miss Pennebaker had, but I could not pinpoint just what. Also, the use of the word *piece* was a puzzle. I could see that the teacher was an attractive female and knew that the word *piece* was used in a figurative sense. But I never fully understood Roy B.'s meaning. My uncertain conclusion was that he wanted to pinch the smooth, lightly tanned flesh of Miss Pennebaker's arm, or maybe her leg.

As far as I know, Roy B. made good on his plan to drop out of school when he reached sixteen. He didn't enroll in school the next year, and I never saw him again. I heard through a classmate he had taken up work at his dad's sawmill. Later someone else reported having seen him picking up roadside trash under the supervision of a sheriff's deputy. Fifty years later, another classmate remembered Roy B. I asked him what happened. He said he didn't know, "Roy B. just rode off to hell one day."

T-Boy's Love Letter

Mr. Willis "T-Boy" Thornton was our neighbor for nearly twenty years. Out of respect, we mostly called him Mr. Willis. But my dad and several neighbors referred to him as T-Boy. No one was sure how the T-Boy name had come about. Some thought it may have been derived from his surname—Thornton—during boyhood days. Others thought the name was really Tea Boy, and that he'd acquired it as an errand boy who delivered jugs of iced tea to his father's field hands.

Regardless of the name, Mr. Willis was a good friend, and we were closer to him than any other neighbor. His farm lay between our farm and a separate tract of land we owned in Brush Creek Bottom. To get to the bottomland, we had to cross his property with tractors and farm implements, and he never had a problem with our trespassing. In summer months, he graciously shared his watermelons with us and traded work with my dad on a day-for-a-day basis once in a while. In winter months, he and my father helped one another cut and split stove wood. If we had to be away from home for a night or two, Mr. Willis milked the cows and performed other chores that needed doing. When he had to be gone from home, we looked after his place and did whatever needed to be done, so the relationship was based on helpfulness, cooperation, and mutual respect.

My mother was fond of his first wife, "Mizz Rosie." As a way of expressing her fondness, she occasionally delivered pies and garden produce across the field that separated our house from theirs. Recipes were sometimes shared, and the two quilted together once in a while. I suppose Mr. Willis and Mizz Rosie were somewhere in their fifties when Mizz Rosie was diagnosed with breast cancer. Surgery failed to cure it or halt its spread, and over time the cancer metastasized to other parts of her body. During the last days of her life, Mama spent nights with her so Mr. Willis could sleep, but she finally died after a brave struggle, and Mr. Willis was left a widower.

Mr. Willis dropped by our house for short visits from time to time, most often during summer months when he could remain outside or on the back porch. His visits continued after Mizz Rosie's death. Late one afternoon, about a year after she had passed, he stopped by. I summoned my dad from the house while T-Boy settled on the ground with his back against the trunk of the big hickory tree that stood on the west side of our house. When Daddy joined him, he commenced to talk about crops and prospects for rain as he took out his crook-stemmed pipe and began to load the bowl with tobacco.

Daddy didn't use tobacco, a fact that probably led me to pay extra-close attention to the pipe-smoking ritual. Mr. Willis kept his tobacco in a tin Prince Albert container that had been carried in the bib of his overalls so long that most of the red paint had worn off.

Over time, the box had taken on the patina of well-used pewter. I knew from previous visits the tobacco in the box was homegrown, not store-bought Prince Albert.

The ritual was always the same: load the pipe, tamp the tobacco with the forefinger, light up, puff a time or two, relax, blink the eyes in a conspicuous manner, and commence to talk about crops and weather. On the day I now reference, Mr. Willis lit his pipe as usual, but I soon detected something unusual was up. He did not segue into conversation in his usual way. Instead of starting to talk about crops and weather, he paused awkwardly, reached into a pocket in the bib of his overalls, and drew out an unopened letter. He passed the letter over to my dad and asked him to open it and read it to him.

Daddy took a long look at the letter. I craned my neck to get a closer look. The return address indicated the letter was from Mrs. Martha Paige, a "widow woman" about Mr. Willis's age. She lived on Shaw Road (the old Boaz Station Road) about two or three miles east of our place, not far from the villages of Boaz and West Viola. After Daddy failed to follow through immediately, T-Boy blinked his eyes in his unique way of conveying mild frustration and said, "Go ahead. Open it up and read it." I was not asked to leave, so I stayed to listen in on whatever Martha Paige had to say to Mr. Willis.

Daddy read the letter aloud. What it said, exactly, I don't recall, but the gist of it was that Miss Martha understood the loneliness Mr. Willis might now be feeling, as she, too, had suffered the loss of a spouse. She indicated she would like to do something to comfort him and suggested he might enjoy one of her homemade pies or just visiting with her sometime. To arrange for a visit, she suggested he phone her in order to settle upon a day and time when they might get together. She closed by saying what a fine reputation Mr. Willis had always enjoyed within the community and affirmed that she shared the community's high opinion of him. When he finished reading, Daddy looked up and said, "Willis, I think she likes you!" T-Boy blinked his eyes and puffed his pipe but said nothing at all in response. Daddy returned his letter to him, assuring him he would make no mention of it except to possibly tell my mother. T-Boy got up to leave, thanked my dad, and ambled back across the field toward home. Later Daddy turned to me, swore me to secrecy, and explained Mr. Willis had never learned to read.

Mr. Willis brought a second letter for my dad to read. I wasn't around to hear it, but not too long afterwards, the neighbors began to notice T-Boy's maroon 1949 Ford was sometimes parked in front of Miss Martha's house on Sunday afternoons. Time led to further escalation of what most neighbors thought was a budding romance, and the couple's association gradually became public knowledge.

Willis and Rosie had had two boys: Charlie and Preston. Charlie, the younger of the two, married Lorenda, a strong-willed, citified sort of woman. When Lorenda got wind of T-Boy's possible courtship of Martha Paige, she became concerned. In the first place, she did not want any disrespect shown toward Rosie, and second, she did not want anyone to interfere with Charlie's ordained right to one day inherit half of T-Boy's farm and other assets. Relations between Martha and Lorenda went from bad to worse after a roadway exchange of words.

One day, Lorenda was driving her nearly new Buick along the

narrow, gravel-strewn Shaw Road when she saw a car coming toward her. Seeing the approaching car and not wanting roadside branches to brush against her shiny car, she found a wide place in the road and eased over to the side. As the approaching car drew near, she noticed the occupants were none other than Martha Paige and her spinster sister, Miriam Gibson. Seeing Lorenda, Miriam brought her car to a stop, rolled down the window, and greeted Lorenda Thornton with a reserved but pleasant "how do you do?" Martha acknowledged Lorenda from her seat opposite the open window but made no eye contact or effort to engage in conversation. This annoyed Lorenda to the point that she suddenly flashed her eyes and said, "Gotta go now, and Martha, don't get too cozy with any widowers."

The affront stung Martha like a bee. "I'll be friends with Willis if I want to," she fired back. "It's a decision we can make without your help! C'mon, Miriam, let's go!" With that, the two cars roared away, spewing rocks behind them.

The apparent courtship continued, but after another year there was still no sign of wedding bells. It was as if things had progressed to a state of comfortable companionship without any indication of an endpoint or climax. Willis and Martha were seen together at church a few times, and Willis's car was seen at Martha's house from time to time. Things didn't seem to be moving along, though. What seemed strange to the neighbors was that Miriam's car was seen in front of T-Boy's house more and more. But looking at it another way, perhaps it was not so strange. Martha didn't drive, and Miriam had always had to chauffeur her to the grocery store, to church, and most other places she went. One neighbor speculated that maybe Martha and

Miriam were redecorating Mr. Willis' house before Martha moved in. Maybe they were getting ready for a wedding without regard to what Lorenda might think or want!

Only a seismologist could have measured the community's shock when a brief notice appeared in the *Mayfield Messenger* announcing the marriage of Mr. Willis Thornton and Miss Miriam Gibson. Apparently, the two had somehow slipped away long enough to take their vows before a justice of the peace and a couple of witnesses. T-Boy later confessed that things had just happened. In the beginning, Martha had depended on her sister to escort her to his house for visits, he said, but as time went on, he found himself drawn more and more toward her younger sister. Furthermore, he added, Miriam turned out to be eager for him to court her.

In hindsight, it is clear that Martha's initial letter to T-Boy set off a chain of events. In the end, many people were affected. In a short time, Lorenda had grown to dislike Martha so much that she actually began to revel in the irony of the situation. "Never take a friend, or a sister, to your favorite fishing hole," she laughed. Seeing Lorenda's selfishness, Charlie's affection for her appeared to wane, and the two eventually became estranged, though they were never divorced. Martha tried to save face by claiming she'd never been interested in Mr. Willis in the first place and that her only involvement with him had been in the role of matchmaker on behalf of her sister. Secretly, however, she began to distance herself from Willis and Miriam. Within a few months, she had learned to drive and had bought a car. T-Boy, in the meantime, puffed contentedly on his pipe but blinked his eyes a bit at the mention of how he'd surprised everyone by marrying Miriam.

Willis and Miriam spent nearly thirty years on the Thornton farm, living in the same house where Rosie had lived. T-Boy survived Miriam by several years and died at age 94. His own survivors included seven grandchildren and a lone son, Preston. Charlie, Lorenda's husband, had died of a heart attack two years before the death of his father. Charlie's widow, Lorenda, survived her father-in-law's death but did not inherit so much as a dime. The farm and all other assets of the Willis Thornton Estate were left to Preston and his heirs.

Sweet Salvation

During the 1950s, Willie Webb preached the Gospel throughout the state of Kentucky. Mr. Willie, as admirers called him, was a compactly built Englishman who could not have been much more than five feet tall. Of course, size is no prerequisite for a preacher, but I always found it surprising that such a small man could command others with such ease and effectiveness. He was to his own sect of believers what Napoleon was to France, a natural leader who exuded self-confidence and power. He was all about business all of the time. Time represented a precious commodity, something to be valued. To him, life was serious and full of purpose. His ramrod-straight posture, deep resonant voice, and penetrating stare commanded the attention of all who knew him.

Mr. Willie was the designated leader of all Kentuckians who were believers in our obscure sect of Christianity, which, for lack of an official name, was simply called "The Truth." The Truth was a protestant group that stressed belief in a literal interpretation of the *Bible* and strict adherence to the teachings of the New Testament.

Ministers of the Gospel were called "Workers." Like the apostles called by Jesus, they entered the ministry, forsaking their homes, earthly possessions, and any hopes for ordinary family life. They went into the world two by two entreating the lost sheep to come home to the safety of the fold.

In the tradition of other Christian sects, believers in The Truth met once a week for Sunday worship and again on Wednesday for prayer meeting. Synagogues, chapels, or other special buildings were not used for Sunday worship. All meetings were held in the homes of members who had "tread the narrow way" long enough to have proved themselves worthy in the sight of God and in the sight of the Workers. In addition to the regular weekly meetings, which typically drew fewer than two dozen souls, there were larger gatherings called conventions.

In Kentucky, two annual conventions were held at separate locations during late summer. These camplike gatherings generally attracted several hundred believers. Each convention consisted of four all-day sessions commencing on Thursday and ending on Sunday. The convention program was set by the Workers. It varied little from convention to convention and always included preaching, singing, and praying as well as long breaks for meals and socialization. Before a convention could begin, the farm where the convention was to be held had to be prepared for the influx of several hundred people. Circus-size tents were erected to serve as meeting and dining halls. Large quantities of food were laid in, barns and outbuildings were cleaned and prepared as sleeping quarters, outdoor toilets were sanitized, and so on.

The biblical basis for conventions was seldom mentioned, but the

Workers emphasized the importance of conventions to the spiritual well-being of all who believed. For those who professed to be saved, conventions were likened to the welcome rain that follows a summer's drought. For nonbelievers, the majority of whom were the children of believers, convention was a time of reaping. It was a time when the unsaved were invited to join the saved in the march against the legions of the devil.

Willie Webb was the master reaper. No one else could present the invitation in such compelling terms. His abilities were not acquired through education for he was not a well-educated man. He certainly had not gone to Oxford or Cambridge. In fact, he had not gone to college at all. He had taken no formal training in rhetoric or homiletics. He had not studied Greek or Hebrew. What he had done, though, was to master the art of emotional oratory. He could effectively evaluate the feelings and thoughts of his listeners. If it is possible for a man of the cloth to be a super salesman, Willie Webb was that person. He knew his clients, and he knew the Scriptures like Sir Isaac Newton knew mathematics.

His abilities were on display once when he visited our home on Penny Corner Road. We were honored beyond measure to have the overseer of the entire state of Kentucky in our home. Consequently, my parents invited local friends and relatives to visit and get to know a man they greatly revered. One relative who came was my dad's oldest brother. Though they considered him unsaved, my parents respected Uncle Harry because they judged him to be reasonable and thoughtful. Over the years, he had pondered many of the profound questions that concern the purpose and meaning of life, and he had come to definite conclusions based on what he reckoned was logical or probable. During Uncle Harry's visit, the conversation somehow turned to religion and salvation. Before anyone knew how or why, he and Willie Webb were engaged in a back-and-forth exchange. Uncle Harry's skepticism and confident manner seemed to unsettle Mr. Willie. As a result, the initial dialogue gradually morphed into a one-sided exchange with Mr. Willie playing the role of preacher. He quoted Scripture, appealed to emotion, reasoned in circles, and finally entangled his adversary in a bewildering barrage of questions and propositions.

Uncle Harry realized the hopelessness of a situation that pitted logic against the unerring authority of Scripture. So he finally excused himself by saying, "Well I've got to go. Mr. Webb, I believe you know your business better than I know mine!" Whether his comment was really a capitulation or just a diplomatic way of ending a hopeless debate is anybody's guess. My dad took it as an admission of his brother's defeat. As the incident was retold, however, it clearly added to Willie Webb's already prodigious reputation as an unassailable authority on religious matters.

I always enjoyed going to conventions until I was about twelve and had reached the "age of accountability." This meant I was old enough to decide my own fate before God. It also meant invitations to the unsaved would henceforth be aimed in my direction. It meant I could no longer sit smugly and comfortably. Gospel sermons and the words of hymns would haunt me, hymns like:

Close to the Kingdom, outside the gate,

Just on the threshold, why longer wait?
Come, take the step tonight,
Let God your heart make right;
Heaven's gate is now in sight,
Why stay away?

It meant if the invitation were to be given, I would have to decide.

In The Truth, the decision to become a Christian was not one to be taken lightly. It meant "walking in newness of life" —that is, leading a new life of prayer and thanksgiving. It meant giving up worldly pleasures. It meant dressing modestly and avoiding movies, televisions, radios, ball games, county fairs, or other amusements. It meant not playing games on Sunday, and of course there could be no gambling, smoking, drinking, or cursing. For farmers, it meant not growing tobacco. For girls, it meant long hair in braids or a bun. It meant not wearing facial makeup. It meant wearing long-sleeved dresses year-round and wearing shoes with no cutouts. It meant segregation from the "worldly throng" and not dating or marrying outside the faith. It meant attending and participating in Gospel meetings, prayer meetings, and Sunday morning meetings. It meant sacrifice and giving a "living testimony" before the world. It meant taking up the cross with Jesus and enduring the scorn of nonbelievers. When one chose to begin walking in "newness of life," it was serious business.

When I turned twelve in June of 1954, I actually thought very little about making my choice for Jesus. But during the convention that followed in September, I became cognizant of my status as an outsider. I remember it well. The invitation was given before the last hymn was sung on Saturday night. Two girls about my age and one very emotional, middle-aged woman stood during the singing of the hymn to signify their acceptance of Jesus Christ as Lord of their lives. I felt a bit uncomfortable during the singing, mainly because several devout believers were craning their necks and peering with the eyes of eagles over the singing crowd. My discomfort was not really too great, though. I rationalized that I had just turned twelve and that an omniscient God must surely know I still had the better part of a year to make my choice.

On the following Sunday, during the last meeting of the convention, everything changed. Willie Webb stepped onto the low platform that served as a pulpit at the front of the meeting tent. Throughout the convention, he had stayed in the background, allowing in-state subordinates and a few visiting out-of-state Workers to feed the flock. The spiritual manna had been plentiful. By this, the fourth day of the convention, temptation seemed far away, and the presence of the Lord seemed very near.

Willie Webb surveyed all who were assembled before him. He knew most of them by name. He had personally converted many of them to Christianity and to The Truth. He had been in their homes and on their farms. He had listened to their troubles and intervened in their squabbles. He had dined with them, preached in their communities, and prayed with them. He knew more than their faces. He knew their ambitions, their weaknesses, and the deepest longings of their hearts. Now he stood on the platform at the front of the tent, ramrod straight. His eyes slowly swept over the assembly, noting the expression on every face. I was nervous. He paused for what seemed like an eternity before he spoke. Willie Webb was the master of the dramatic pause. Every eye was upon him. The only sounds were a few muffled coughs and the distant cry of a baby somewhere outside the tent.

At last he spoke with such suddenness and volume that I must have flinched a bit. "The Lord has been good these four days. He has spread a bountiful table before us, and we have eaten until we are full. He has spoken to our hearts, quickened our minds and spirits, and moved us to make new vows. He has given us favorable weather. He has watched over us and preserved us. We have much to be thankful for." He paused to let his words sink in. "Some of you," he continued, "will leave these hallowed grounds, go back to your homes, and fight the good fight of faith. Many of you will leave these grounds by automobile. Be careful. The highways are treacherous. A person's life can be taken in a moment's notice. It makes no difference if you are young or old. Your life can be snuffed out in an instant, and you will stand before the Lord in the Day of Judgment. I feel that there are some here with whom the Lord has been speaking but who as yet have not made the choice to serve Him."

At that moment, I realized Willie Webb was going to test the meeting. I also realized I was uneasy and chilly. "We are going to sing a hymn in closing," he announced. "When we get to the last verse, if there is anyone who wishes to repent and give control of your heart and life to Jesus, please indicate your intentions by standing to your feet and remain standing until the entire hymn has been sung." I was eager to move on, but I could not speed things up. Willie Webb was in control, and he now paused to read aloud the words of the last verse of the hymn he had chosen:

> *Lord Jesus, teach me how to choose,*
> *I'm glad that thou dost understand*
> *The struggle of the youthful heart,*
> *The snares that lie on every hand;*
> *And tho' I do not grasp it now,*
> *Better I'll know when life is done,*
> *Why Thou didst point the hardest path,*
> *Ask'd me the straightest course to run.*

When he finished the last verse, he did not stop. Instead, he continued on through the chorus:

> *Lord Jesus, teach me how to choose,*
> *Talk Thou with me these choices o'er.*
> *Then let me choose as I would choose,*
> *When time and seasons are no more.*

My anxiety was growing by the minute, and I was ready to sing, but Mr. Willie was not ready to sing. He recalled how Jesus had sacrificed his all on the middle cross of Calvary. He recalled how our parents and the Workers had sacrificed, too. Even though I deliberately tried to distract myself, I found that his words were going straight to my heart. I began to recall things as he talked. I remembered my parents' teachings and our family *Bible* readings. I remembered their love and concern for my soul. I also remembered the concern the Workers had shown. I recalled stories we had shared, fishing trips together, and walks we had taken. I recalled how one of the sister Workers had helped me cover an old wooden case in Naugahyde so I would be able to have my own suitcase for convention. I was unable to escape. It was as though I were floundering in a rushing river and being drawn into a watery vortex by the words that came from the platform. All at once, Willie Webb seemed to be preaching, beseeching, and firing dire warnings all at the same time. The cadence of his oration was rhythmic and mesmerizing. His voice was like a drumbeat at times. At other times, the rhythm was interrupted as he paused to gently entreat, plead, and pluck every string of emotion in my youthful heart.

Finally, he again turned his attention to the unsung hymn. After repeating the invitation in a most persuasive manner, we began to sing. At first, the sound of the mingled voices was sweet, even reassuring. But as we approached the beginning of the last verse, I again became aware of my own misery and indecision. As we began the last verse, a number of troubled, weeping souls stood to their feet, so many in fact that the scene conjured up the image of popcorn over a hot fire. I began to experience a degree of relief. The large number of new converts would ensure no one would notice I had not stood.

When the singing ended, Mr. Willie asked those who had stood to be seated. I was sure it was over, but I was wrong. Instead of praying a final prayer and dismissing, he paused and surveyed the assembly again. This time I was sure that he was looking straight at me! His gaze was penetrating. It seemed as if it penetrated to the "dividing asunder of bone and marrow" and to the "thoughts and intents of the heart." After another pause, he said, "There may still be some among us who have not yielded their hearts to God. Jesus is interceding for you at this very moment. He is on God's right hand. He knows your struggles. He knows that Satan is trying to beguile you. He knows that he is trying to keep you from making the choice that will lead to greater earthly satisfaction now and to eternal life later on. We are going to sing the last stanza of this hymn again. If you are willing to make Jesus your Lord, please stand to your feet."

We began to sing the mournful, agonizing verse again. As we neared the end, no one had stood. I shifted my weight forward to stand to my feet. But as I did, the muscles in my legs began to tremble, my confidence waned, and instead of rising, I shifted in my seat, and at last the singing was over. Sweat was beaded on my forehead and upper lip. Willie Webb dismissed the gathering with a prayer. I numbly made my way out of the tent, hardly noticing as friends said goodbye.

Two years later, on the same convention grounds, I stood to my feet. It was on a Saturday night. I had to do it. The thought of being unsaved when Willie Webb presented the invitation on the following day was more than I could bear.

Hannah's Quilt

Hannah Kerrigan and her cousin Ruthie Hainsworth whispered quietly beneath the quilt that formed a roof over their heads. Being only nine and eight years old, respectively, they were considered too young to join in the quilting with the five women who were gathered around the big, rectangular quilting frame. The frame, suspended by four hooks in the ceiling of the living room, was positioned only thirty inches or so above floor level. The two girls sat cross-legged in the shadows playing with rag dolls. It was winter, and there was a fire in the big, fieldstone fireplace at the north end of the room. The warmth of the fire, the faint whistle of the tea kettle from somewhere in the nearby kitchen, and conversations among the quilters wrapped the girls in a blanket of comfort and security. Between periods of play, Hannah and Ruthie whispered and giggled, mostly about large legs, cotton stockings, and lace-up shoes that projected into the space under the quilt. Only occasionally did the girls eavesdrop on the conversations above. And when they did, they didn't listen for long. Conversations about the weather, work to be done, men folks, recipes, quilt patterns, and personal recollections about the bits of material being sewn did not hold the interest of Hannah and Ruthie.

Their interest was in dolls and active play.

During the winter months, the quilting scene was often repeated at the Kerrigan home and at others like it in Larue County, Kentucky. For women in rural communities, quilting was both a useful activity and a means of relaxation. Everyone enjoyed the socialization it provided, including the children. When a girl got to be about eleven or twelve years old, she was expected to join in the quilting, at least for short periods of time, and by the time she reached thirteen or fourteen, she was expected to fully join in with the older women.

As she grew older, Hannah became less and less interested in quilting. There were enjoyable moments, of course, but generally she found the company of the older women boring. Too often their outlook was tradition-bound, even closed-minded, she thought. Though others complimented her quilting, pointing out the tiny, uniform stitches she made, her heart was not in it. Her mind drifted to faraway places, nice clothes, dreams of college, and city life.

By 1935, the year Hannah turned sixteen, it was no longer considered fashionable, even among the tradition-bound folk of Larue County, to announce a young woman's availability for marriage by holding a quilting bee in her honor. But Hannah's mother, Agnes Kerrigan, and her aunt, Sarah Farley, were not concerned with emerging social customs. They were old-fashioned and proud of it! Young girls had benefited from quiltings as long as either of them could remember, and they saw no need to change things.

Hannah looked mature for sixteen. Many people guessed her to be twenty. Her comely appearance, pleasant way of interacting with others, and refined manners had resulted in her being teased more than a little about the local lads who eyed her during church services. She understood the teasing, yet it never failed to make her uncomfortable. Hannah was not interested in "getting hitched," to use the local euphemism, and what logically followed was that a special quilting was not needed. Despite her expressed wishes, Hannah found that her mother was determined to hold a quilting in her honor. The way Agnes looked at it, Hannah was getting close to the age at which she should marry, and she deserved a quilting whether she wanted one or not!

Years ago, Agnes Kerrigan had made up her mind that Hannah's quilt would be something special. Hannah had always been a special child. She was polite, obedient, keen-minded, and pretty. Over the years, Agnes had secretly saved and pieced together tiny scraps of the fabrics that had clothed the family since she had married Jeremiah in 1914, the year the Great War broke out in Europe. By looking at the scraps now pieced together, she could recount much of the family history over the past twenty-one years. There were pieces from Willie's handmade shirts, one that he had worn when he started to school. Willie was her firstborn, and there were many examples of his garments throughout the quilt top. Literally thousands of tiny pieces of cloth had been pieced together to form the blocks of an unusual pattern known as the Exploding Fan. Many pieces were no more than two inches long and no wider than a thimble. Included were pieces from practically everything Hannah had ever worn. But that was not all. There were pieces of Agnes's own garments and those of the younger children: Mary, Margaret, and little Charles. Behind every piece there was a story, and Agnes Kerrigan knew every story. Each time she looked at the quilt top, the memories returned.

She was not overly concerned with Hannah's objection to the quilting. Hannah often talked about fancy clothes, city life, and going to college, but deep down Agnes knew Hannah was a sensible girl. It was just a stage she was going through. She would outgrow her foolhardy ambitions in a year or two. She would find a good, steady boy and settle down to raise a family of her own.

Times were hard in 1935. Prices for farm goods, including the Kerrigan's main crop, tobacco, were at rock bottom. People said Roosevelt would get the country moving again, but no one could tell just when. Jeremiah had said that if things didn't get better, Hannah might have to drop out of high school for a while. The thought terrified her.

Hannah loved school. Moreover, she knew her only hope of escaping poverty and the slow-paced life of Larue County was to stay in school. Perhaps if she finished high school she would be able to find a job in an office in Louisville or Cincinnati. An even better thought was the idea of going to college, but she didn't let herself think about that too much. College would cost money, and money was hard to come by. Besides, it was tough for a woman to gain admission to a college. Nevertheless, Hannah held on to faint hope and focused on excelling in her schoolwork.

In 1937, Hannah Louise Kerrigan became the first member of her family to graduate from high school. She had taken Latin, algebra, rhetoric, world geography, and other subjects that left relatives in awe of her. As she gave the valedictory address at the commencement ceremony, Agnes' pride in her daughter's accomplishments gave way to a foreboding sense of uncertainty, even fear. Ever since Hannah's quilting two years ago, Agnes had kept her worst fears in the deepest recesses of her mind. Now, as Hannah stood confidently before her teachers, classmates, and others, the fears worked their way to the surface. What if Hannah didn't find a good boy to marry? So far, she hadn't had a serious suitor although several young men had shown interest. Sure, boys had walked her home from church a few times, but Hannah never seemed excited. Memories of the day of Hannah's quilting flashed into her mind. She remembered how upset Hannah had been when she had steadfastly insisted on having the quilting. She recalled entering Hannah's quilt in a competition at the county fair. It had taken first prize, including a three-dollar cash award, but Hannah had shown little interest and insisted the prize money was not hers. "It's your quilt, Mama," she had said, "and I'm not taking the three dollars." Agnes reckoned Hannah somehow felt acceptance of the quilt meant acceptance of the idea of marriage.

Hannah left for Louisville shortly after graduation but returned three days later unable to find work. Agnes was relieved at first; however, relief turned to guilt as she recalled the disappointment in Hannah's eyes as she stepped off the train in Elizabethtown. She didn't share her daughter's dreams, but it was painful to see them crushed. Several days later, Hannah was alive with new hope. A former teacher had contacted her about taking an exam that could qualify her for a scholarship at Transylvania University. It would mean going to Lexington, and that meant more transportation and travel costs. One night's lodging in a dormitory room would be provided, according to the teacher. That would certainly help.

Hannah knew her parents had already borne the costs of a train ticket to Louisville and that they had sacrificed for years to see her through high school. She was reluctant to ask more of them. Still, she couldn't conceal her excitement, nor could she ignore such an opportunity. After a lengthy family discussion, her father announced he would get the money so she could go, but he made it clear that if things didn't work out in Lexington, she should understand she would have to come back home to help the younger children stay in school.

Four years had passed since she had set out to take the exam in Lexington. It had been the four most rewarding years of her life. She had learned a lot. She had become increasingly aware of the world around her and of her own humanity. She had reached a new acme. She had graduated from Transylvania *cum laude*, with a major in geography and minors in history and French. Success had been accompanied by sacrifice, however. The scholarship had provided tuition, but she had also worked part time, and the family had taken a second mortgage on the farm to help during her last year. She thought of her mother and how time and divergent interests had distanced them from one another. When Agnes came to Lexington for Hannah's graduation, she talked hopefully about a teaching post that was open in Larue County. She also expressed frustration at not being able to find Hannah's quilt. Hannah cringed with guilt at the mention of the quilt and lied when her mother asked if she knew where it might be. Hannah hated to lie but did so anyway. She couldn't tell her mother the truth right now. Maybe someday.

The truth was that she had brought the quilt to Transylvania after spending the Christmas break at home. It was during her senior year just a few months back. Because it was cold in her dormitory room, she had packed it to bring back to Lexington without thinking to tell her mother. Later, the house director at the dormitory had noticed it on her bed and commented on it. When Hannah dismissed the compliment in a casual way, the director assumed the quilt meant little to Hannah. Knowing that Hannah was in need of money, she mentioned she had a friend who collected handmade quilts. Blinded by the need for money, Hannah agreed to let the house director's friend look at the quilt. Mrs. Clay, the collector, turned out to be a disarming sort of lady who could read the facial expressions of others like an open book. When she had arrived, Hannah had asked eight dollars for the quilt, but when the lady bargained for seven dollars, Hannah gave in.

After graduation, Hannah did not return to Larue County. Instead she accepted a fellowship to study international commerce at New York University. After receiving her master's degree a year later, she took a position in Washington, DC as a staff researcher with Warren and Stone, a law firm specializing in international tariff and trade regulations. World War II had broken out before she had arrived turning the city into a beehive of political and commercial activity. During her interview for the job, she met Seth Warren III, then a junior partner in the firm.

Within a year, the two were married. Seth's parents were respectful, but Hannah sensed their disappointment when Seth introduced her as his bride-to-be. No doubt they would have liked someone from a prominent East Coast family. Partly out of deference to the Warrens, and partly because she did not want to confront her mother about the missing quilt, Hannah proposed a simple wedding with minimal publicity and no out-of-town guests. She was not sure what the Warrens would make of her simple, country folk, and she was also apprehensive about how her own relatives might react. But the Warrens insisted that the wedding involve the Kerrigans and that they come to Washington for the wedding. The wedding had gone well, and Hannah had been surprised at how well her parents and siblings had interacted with the more sophisticated Warrens. Agnes had brought several things from Hannah's "hope chest" and inquired again about the missing quilt. Overwhelmed by guilt, Hannah confessed that she might have taken it to Transylvania. Maybe it had somehow been lost or stolen, she said. Agnes Kerrigan gave her daughter a long, doubtful look but said nothing.

After the long, agonizing years of World War II, time passed swiftly. Hannah's life became a whirl: meetings with attorneys and officials from abroad, formal meals and parties, business travel, and hurried holidays. Now a senior partner of the firm, Seth was sometimes gone for extended periods of time. In the midst of the rush, their only child, Seth IV, born in 1945, grew up quickly. It was hard to fathom that he was already in college at Princeton.

When her father died in 1965, Hannah returned to Larue County for the funeral and to spend a few days with her mother. Despite the occasion, she was surprised by how much she enjoyed the visit and by the resilience and tough-mindedness of her mother. A new wing had been added to the old log part of the house, and the rooms were tastefully furnished with antiques and folk art. Having acquired a recent interest in folk art herself, she enjoyed talking to her mother about hand-loomed textiles, quilts, whirligigs, salt-glazed pottery, and the like.

When she got back to Washington, Hannah thought back to the 1930s and the sacrifices her father had made for the family. As she relived the visit with her mother after the funeral, it hit her for the first time that she had made no mention of the quilt, even though they had talked a great deal about such things. For the first time in her life, Hannah wished she had the quilt her mother and friends had made for her. She decided she would go to Lexington at the first opportunity to see if she could locate it.

After Princeton, Seth Warren IV finished law school at the University of Virginia and joined the family firm in Washington. He married a delightful young woman whom Hannah adored. Victoria, or Vickie as they called her, was from the small town of Georgetown, Kentucky. Seth met her when she came to Washington as an aide to Senator John Sherman Cooper. Being from Kentucky made Vickie special to Hannah.

For years, the Warrens had resided in the Washington suburb of Georgetown, and Vickie loved to joke that she had always felt at home at the Warrens'—Georgetown had always been home! Vickie's passion was politics, but she had other interests, including the art, music, and dance traditions of people from Southern Appalachia. Her interest in mountain people and their customs was another reason Hannah enjoyed the company of her daughter-in-law.

After Hannah made several unsuccessful attempts to locate her quilt, Vickie became interested in helping her find it. Vickie learned there was to be a large arts and crafts show in Berea, Kentucky, and suggested it might be interesting because quilt making was to be featured. Soon plans were made to visit Vickie's relatives in Georgetown, stay at Boone Tavern in Berea, and snoop around Lexington a bit. After flying to Kentucky, they arranged for a rental car and were soon enjoying Berea. There they saw potters at work, dulcimers being crafted, brooms being made, displays of quilts, split-oak baskets being woven, and other reminders of the past. They even attended a seminar on the early settlement of Southern Appalachia and learned how traditional arts and crafts had evolved over the years.

Once, Hannah made a headlong rush toward a quilt display when she thought she saw her quilt. When Vickie caught up to her, she found Hannah looking with disappointment at a fine quilt made in the Exploding Fan design. It was not her quilt, she told Vickie, but there was much about it that reminded her of it. At the center was a circle made of narrow strips of material joined together. Extending outward, like points of a compass, were individual blocks comprising the same narrow strips of material arranged to form half-circles, each resembling a partly open folding fan. Between the four rows of blocks that radiated from the central circle toward the quilt's edge were other blocks consisting of smaller, quarter-circles, again constructed of tiny strips of fabric sewn together to resemble a partially open fan.

Although the Berea quilt was of the same basic pattern as her quilt, Hannah noted several differences. The stitching was good but not as fine as that in her quilt. There were seven or eight stitches per inch rather than the nine to ten stitches per inch her mother had insisted upon. The border lacked the intricate design she remembered from her quilt. And of course, the quilt lacked the special scraps of material Agnes had collected over the years, scraps that made her quilt truly unique. But the quilt in front of Hannah was for sale, and she bought it for $250. It did, after all, resemble the quilt she had let slip away on that fateful day in early 1941.

Before returning to the airport in Louisville, Hannah and Vickie had planned to go by Transylvania. There, they hoped to find someone Hannah had known who could provide a clue as to the whereabouts of the quilt. At Transy, they were disappointed to learn that Hannah's old house director had retired to Florida but were pleasantly surprised to encounter Regina Dibbs. Regina, whose last name was now Baldwin, had been a classmate at Transylvania. Now, they discovered, she had returned to her alma mater as a faculty member in the art department. Pottery was her specialty, they learned, but she seemed to know a good deal about old textiles, fiber art, sculpture, and many other kinds of art.

Regina was so cordial and full of conversation they insisted she join them for lunch. Over soup and sandwiches, they talked about old times and things they had seen in Berea. Regina filled Hannah in on all kinds of news about former classmates and faculty members.

On the ride back to campus, Regina spotted the quilt Hannah had bought in Berea and commented on it. Noting Regina's interest, Hannah inquired: "Do you remember the one I had that I sold to some lady the house director knew?"

"No," Regina responded, "but I'll tell you where I saw one that reminds me of this one."

"Where?" Hannah asked.

"At The Speed in Louisville," she replied.

After they dropped Regina off at Transylvania, they headed to Louisville for the trip home. With almost four hours before their flight back to Washington, Vickie insisted they visit the J. B. Speed Museum before going home. Hannah was reluctant at first, fearing further disappointment. But in the end, Vickie won out, and they arrived at the museum a short time later.

At Hannah's request, the attendant at the admissions desk directed them to the ongoing display of early Kentucky quilts. Each quilt was displayed in a large, well-lighted booth against a white background. A description of each quilt's origin, design, and history was displayed under a clear, Lucite panel. It didn't take long for Hannah's eye to settle upon the quilt Regina had spoken of. As she drew closer, tears welled up in her eyes. It was her quilt! A strange feeling swept over her. The experience was almost unreal—almost surreal. She examined the description to be sure It read:

An exquisite example of a quilt in the Exploding Fan pattern.

Circa 1935. Exceptionally fine needlework. Top consists of more than 3,600 separate pieces. Attributed to the Kerrigan family of Hardin County, Kentucky.

The minor error in attribution did not concern her in the least. It was her quilt. Memories flooded back. There was the navy polka dot that had been her mother's skirt and the gray stripe that had been her father's shirt. There was the tiny, flowered calico of the puffed sleeves and ruffled hem of a dress she had worn when she started school. There were many other pieces that were a part of her growing up including bits from clothes Willie, Mary, Margaret, and Charles had worn. Suddenly she snapped out of the surreal world of the past, her mind regaining its focus.

She rushed to the attendant's desk eager to learn who was in charge of acquisitions. The attendant said a Mr. Woodall was in charge. He added, however, that the quilt collection on display did not belong to the museum. The displayed quilts were on loan from the collection of William "Bill" Schroeder and his wife, Meredith, of Paducah, Kentucky. The return trip to Washington was a mix of relief at having found the quilt of her youth and the frustration of not being able to regain ownership. As they flew, Hannah pondered a return trip to Kentucky.

In the weeks that followed, Hannah corresponded with the Schroeders. She learned that The Speed would return the quilt to the Schroeders in November of that year, 1973. She also learned the quilt's present owners were not currently considering deaccessioning any quilt from their collection, but they would be willing to meet with Hannah to discuss the quilt's history and to offer her the "first right of refusal" in case a later decision was made to sell. Hannah made arrangements to meet with the Schroeders and traveled to Paducah to personally tell the story of the quilt, to correct the minor error in attribution, and to try to sway Bill and Meredith Schroeder to sell the quilt.

It was a chilly day in early December when Hannah arrived in Paducah. The Schroeders turned out to be genteel southerners with the business savvy of New York bankers. That they later cofounded the National Quilt Museum and became nationwide leaders in the quilt community did not surprise Hannah in the least. The Schroeders were zealots when it came to quilts and quilting.

Meredith indicated she and her husband had purchased the quilt from Mrs. Hilda Clay of Lexington, Kentucky. She did not indicate a purchase price. She then summarized their objectives as collectors, indicating that they generally did not sell quilts from their collection and that they had therefore not entertained the possibility of deaccessioning Hannah's quilt. If it were to be sold, she continued, they would likely assign it to a public auction house, such as Sotheby's. Hannah was not encouraged, nor was she deterred. There was hope.

When it was her turn to speak, Hannah retold the story of how she had initially failed to appreciate the quilt and described the conditions under which she had given it up. To highlight her seriousness, she drew attention to her association with the law firm of Warren and Stone and noted the firm had a long history of patronizing the arts. She ended by requesting that the Schroeders have the quilt evaluated by a qualified appraiser and that the appraisal be used as a guide to set a sales price. The Schroeders listened and indicated they would consider her request but made no promises.

In March of 1974, a certified letter arrived from Bill and Meredith Schroder. It proposed a sales price of $1,400 for the quilt with the understanding that Hannah would assist in finding a suitable replacement for the Schroeder Collection. After an additional exchange of letters and phone calls, Hannah returned to Paducah with the quilt she had bought in Berea and exchanged it and the agreed-upon $1,400 for the quilt of her youth. Having previously learned of the Schroeders' dream of founding a quilt museum, she presented a separate check in the amount of $10,000. The check was from Warren and Stone, she explained, adding that its use was restricted to the promotion of "quilt preservation and quilt appreciation" on a national level.

The acquisition came none too soon. The quilt had been in the possession of others for almost thirty-three years. Two weeks later, Willie contacted her with news that their mother was seriously ill with pneumonia. Hannah boarded the first plane for Louisville, packing the quilt in a separate carry-on case. When she got to Larue County, she found her mother weak and barely able to speak. She regretted that it had taken so long and that it had to be in the present situation, but after seeing her mother, she could not wait to unfurl the quilt. When she did, she saw a glimmer of new life in her eyes. "I didn't think you had it anymore," she whispered. Hannah smiled back, grasped her mother's hand, and held it for a long time.

Within weeks, her mother, then 78 years old, made a remarkable recovery. Hannah remained with her throughout her recovery and enjoyed many long conversations about her childhood and growing up in Kentucky. And for the first time, Hannah recounted the whole story of the quilt. When she left for Washington, the bond with her mother had never been stronger. Twenty-three months later, Agnes Kerrigan, fourscore years in age, suffered a fatal heart attack. She had been working in her flowerbeds alongside the log portion of the house where the quilt frames had hung.

When the estate was settled, Hannah's brother, Charles, negotiated with the remaining heirs to buy the farmland. Hannah became the owner of the house and garden. For years afterward, the old home place became a seasonal retreat: a place of refuge and rest. There was something about just lolling in the recliner in the quietness of the living room, staring up at the hooks in the ceiling, listening to the crackle of the fire, and dreaming.

Uncle Melvin

My great-uncle Melvin Reasons lived alone in a weather-grayed farmhouse that sat on a hill within sight of my grandparents' house. I turned fifteen the day before he died. A neighbor found him lying on his manicured lawn, still grasping a long-handled awl he had used to spear fallen leaves. The year was 1957, a date I now associate with Sputnik, technological growth, and a rise in consumerism and materialism. Around that time, people in our neck of the woods became increasingly obsessed with owning all sorts of newfangled consumer devices, which of course made life easier in some ways but at the same time also made it more complex and hurried.

Uncle Melvin quietly rejected the rush for change and all that was modern in his day. He had no electricity, no refrigeration, no running water, and no indoor plumbing. He had no radio, no television, no phonograph, no stereo or telephone, and of course no digital technology of any kind. He never maintained a bank account and never sought nor had any sort of public employment. Although he attended church once in a while, he never belonged to a church group or any other organized group. He was friendly and sociable but kept to himself for the most part. On occasion, he walked the two-mile distance to Shaw, a crossroads community where groceries were sold.

My grandmother or one of the nieces still living at home delivered his lunch every day, but he otherwise made do on his own. He never ate at a restaurant, never attended a ballgame or concert, never attended a political rally, and as far as I know never voted in an election. He had no wife, no children, no automobile, no motorized farm machinery, and no mortgage. He was, in short, the most unencumbered man I ever knew. Despite all he did without, he always seemed happy, healthy, and agreeable.

Uncle Melvin's possessions were few and simple. He owned a nickel-plated pocketwatch he kept attached to the bib of his denim overalls by means of a braided leather thong. He had a couple of pocketknives with blades of Solingen steel. These he put to use in carving treenware and cleverly conceived holders for pencils and matches. His porch and house were furnished with simple chairs and benches he fashioned by hand. He always kept a sharp, well-oiled, reel lawn mower—a Bluegrass—and an assortment of rakes and grass clippers, all of which were used to manicure his summer lawn. He had a collection of well-maintained axes, hoes, froes, wood saws, and other hand tools. His most-prized possession was a matched team of draft horses he employed in cultivating small patches of corn and tobacco as cash crops. Uncle Melvin took pride in his horses, and his team was invariably outfitted with good-quality leather harnesses adorned with brass buttons, shiny buckles, and brightly dyed tassels.

Most of our visits to Uncle Melvin's were in conjunction with my mother's barber work. Although he had a straight razor for shaving, Uncle Melvin depended on my mother to cut his hair. Hair-cutting visits were drawn-out affairs that doubled as social visits. Typically, our entire family—four or five of us then—would arrive at his house shortly before dark. He would welcome us and immediately commence to lead us on a tour of his yard and wood lot. As we ambled about, Uncle Melvin would display things he had made, call attention to improvements in and around the yard, and point out birds' nests he had recently discovered. In good weather, the tour ended on his porch where he and my parents would continue conversations about the weather, prospects for crops, and news about neighbors and relatives. My mother would cut his hair as they talked using a pair of scissors, a comb, and a prized set of hand-operated clippers from Sears and Roebuck.

In cold weather, we skipped the porch to move inside where mother would perform the hair-cutting ritual by the light of a kerosene lamp. I don't remember how the haircuts came out, but I do remember the dimness of the room as well as passing the time by watching shadows of my mother as she moved. Uncle Melvin always appreciated our visits and insisted on paying for his haircuts. Though reluctant, Mother always accepted his fifty cents, but only after protesting and saying he'd only needed "a trim."

In thinking back to "Uncle Melvin days," other memories come to mind. For instance, I remember him saying he'd "heered" this or that. I remember his chuckles and that they ended with a high-pitched "heee!" I recall the story of his having lost his father at thirteen and how he and my grandfather, then eleven, had later cultivated and harvested that year's crop. Still another memory that remains with me relates to my grandparents' practice of passing on the daily newspaper to Uncle Melvin after they'd finished reading it. I well recall how much he enjoyed the comic strips and political cartoons. After his death, neighbors could hardly believe it when Uncle Melvin's life savings were found in a hollowed-out niche in one of the logs in the barn that stood back of his house. The barn is gone now. So is the house, and so is Uncle Melvin, except for the memories.

Years later, I stood alone in the yard Uncle Melvin used to mow near the spot where he lay on June 3, 1957. I was there to revisit him, to kindle the tinder of old memories, and to reflect upon his life. Some might ask: "Why bother? He was a bystander who never really lived." But I don't buy that interpretation. It is true his impact was not great by the usual standards for measuring people and their contributions to the world. Only a few people knew him, and even fewer knew him well. He never sought recognition or publicity. He never acquired wealth or power. He ignored fads and trends but never faulted others for embracing them. He was happy to blend with nature rather than to leave his mark upon it. He made no contribution to the landfills that stand as monuments to the lives of others. He consumed few of the world's resources, preferring the lifestyle espoused by Thoreau, whom incidentally he had never read. His simple ways left the world much as he had found it. After his death, there was little evidence of his coming and going. But to me, there was a special beauty about Uncle Melvin's life. It was like a snowflake born in the heavens to fall silently through the air, softly kiss the ground, and melt away.

Mountain Dancer

I vividly recall the day we encountered the girl we would later call the "mountain dancer." My wife and I had arrived at the Museum of Appalachia near Norris, Tennessee, on a return trip from North Carolina. The sky was obscured by low-hanging clouds that bespoke the prospect of rain. Redbud blossoms dried and faded on flocked limbs even as dogwood buds opened in early bloom. The forest was awakening; winter was faltering. The warm breath of spring stirred somewhere to the South.

We arrived at the museum in early afternoon in time to enjoy the folk art, including a range of one-of-a-kind devices designed to fulfill some whimsy or special need of a now-lost lifestyle. We hurried past haystacks, iron salt kettles, and a collection of watering troughs made from huge, hewn-out logs. But the weather caught up with us as a light rain began to fall. Spotting shelter under the dogtrot of a nearby log house, we headed for cover.

There we found a couple engaged in a conversation with a museum docent. Predictably, they were talking about mountain culture and must-see displays at the museum. The interpreter was at ease, leaning comfortably against the log wall, his straight chair tilted back on two legs. As my eyes adjusted to the dimness of the cloud-darkened dogtrot, I could see he was holding a fiddle, an instrument I loved but one that mountain preachers considered sin-inducing: the Devil's Box, they called it. Engrossed in conversation, the interpreter made a gesture toward me as we joined the group.

Suddenly the spring shower let loose in full force. Visitors caught outside began to scatter and run for cover. A young woman sprinted in our direction and joined us in the dogtrot. Understandably, she was a bit winded from her run, and as she paused to catch her breath I noticed her unblemished skin and the raindrops that fell into beads along her neck. She was of average height. Her body was slender and beguiling, its curves partially hidden beneath her dress. Her hazel eyes flashed briefly around the dogtrot, though she mostly averted them from the stares of others as she began to rearrange strands of her now-disheveled hair. I guessed she was in her twenties, but she might have been in her late teens. After acknowledging the group with a hint of a smile as if apologizing for intruding, she moved to stand along the wall opposite that of the elderly interpreter who by now had noticed the sudden commotion and the roar of the rain.

Seeing he had a captive audience, the interpreter positioned the fiddle under his chin and without introduction proceeded to play a couple of melancholy tunes that reminded me of bagpipes, free-range sheep, and the Highlands of my ancestors. Everyone listened attentively. After his last number, he paused to welcome everyone to the museum and to ask if anyone had a request that he might play. With that small invitation, the woman who had been there from the start suggested, "Old Joe Clark," up-tempo, she added. The old man began to play, his bow shuffling rapidly over the fiddle strings, his fingers walking delicately along the neck of the instrument. The beat was strong even without the accompaniment of a bass or other rhythm maker.

To my surprise, and I believe to the surprise of everyone there, the young girl sprang from her position along the wall and into the middle of the dogtrot. There was no shyness about her now. Instantly, she picked up the beat and began to dance with uninhibited exuberance, the movements of her body seeming to fill the dogtrot. The worn boards flexed and moved and thumped under her feet. Lightly tanned legs disappeared beneath the hemline of her cotton dress, which rose and fell as she moved and, though not tightly fitted, revealed flashes of her thighs. The force of her feet on the floorboards produced a pleasant thump much like that of a bass fiddle. When the music ended, the small audience applauded robustly and complimented the girl on her performance. She appeared not to be embarrassed by the attention and was only slightly winded, but when the fiddler played again, she did not dance. Soon the shower subsided, and we said our goodbyes to those who remained.

The whole song and dance had not lasted long. What made it so special is hard to say. The undeniable comeliness of the girl was one thing, of course, but it was more than that. Perhaps it was a combination of things: the historic setting, the rhythm and melody of the music, the rain, *and* the girl in her simple attire. Maybe it was the sheer energy of the dance and the spontaneity of it all. One thing is certain, though: It was an unforgettable dance, one I wished my old friend John Patten could have been there to see. It was a performance that could never be repeated and, even if it could, would serve little purpose. Something would be lost.

Happily, the day I met the mountain dancer lives on in my mind, stored in the guarded recesses of memory among the great masterpieces of art, stored with other random but perfect collisions of matter and energy in time and space.

Lesson Learned

During the 1960s, I was employed as a science teacher in Scott County, Missouri, an area close to the Mississippi River in the southeastern part of the state. The school where I taught was located toward the west end of a *Strassendorf*-like town that had once been called Fornfelt but had been renamed Scott City right after World War II. I enjoyed my position as a young teacher and the respect the community afforded teachers, especially science teachers.

During the summer of 1964, my young wife and I moved into town about a month before the beginning of the school year. As a part of getting settled, I stopped by the Scott City Bank to open an account. When I gave my name to the banker and announced I wanted to open a new account, he immediately inquired, "Aren't you the new science teacher?" I answered affirmatively, feeling a surge of self-importance. Two thoughts immediately came to mind: first, this is a place where word gets around quickly, and second, it is also a place where teachers are respected. Time proved both impressions to be correct.

The Scott City community turned out to be progressive but, at the same time, respectful of tradition. Demographically, most students were of German descent. Their surnames gave the secret away: Dannenmueller, Albrecht, Sherer, Klughart, Dahms, Menz, Katzmueller, and so on. Their parents and grandparents were religious folks, generally Roman Catholic or Lutheran, who led lives that balanced Christian piety with a spark of the fun-loving spirit of Oktoberfest. Their core values were a deep belief in discipline, individual accountability, and the liberating power of science and technology (it was the Age of Sputnik). Most were not highly educated, but they respected teachers and schools and were determined that their children would have the opportunity to obtain a first-rate education. Coming from Kentucky, where basketball and cheerleading were often glorified, I was surprised to learn the school superintendent gave an account of the successes of recent graduates to the general public on an annual basis.

Science and mathematics teachers in the high school were awarded a head coach's salary supplement in exchange for a willingness to "coach" the preparation of science fair projects during after-school hours. This duty and my additional role as Science Club sponsor allowed me to develop teacher-student relationships beyond the classroom. As I have said, I was young at the time. Consequently, I possessed a good deal of energy along with a voracious appetite for science and learning. Students gravitated to me. Under my guidance, our students won unprecedented numbers of awards at the Regional Science Fair in Cape Girardeau, and two students, Margaret Gibson and John Howard Moore, garnered recognition that allowed them to enter projects in the National Science Fair. It may border on bragging, but I don't think it would be an exaggeration to say that many students saw me as a guru and model of sorts.

The *Bible* says "pride goes before a fall." This oft-cited proverb certainly applies in my case. Before I get into specifics, though, I should note I came to be seen as a local authority on matters of science, someone who could be relied upon to answer questions posed by students, colleagues, or members of the community. Once, for example, a parent brought me a jar containing the whitish, ribbon-like remains of something that was noticably segmented. A dog had purportedly passed the specimen in his feces. I correctly identified the remains as being those of a common tapeworm, *Diphyllobothrium latum*.

Another time, a student presented me with a tiny fly and wanted to know what it was called. After examining it under a dissecting microscope, I reported that it was a fruit fly of some sort but not the well-know variety, *Drosophila melanogaster.* It was similar, I conceded. However, the fly's overall size and the venation pattern in its membranous wings led me to believe it might be some other fruit fly, possibly *Drosophila virilus.* Dipteran flies, I noted, were particularly difficult to identify to the species level, and thus I couldn't make a more precise identification.

On still another occasion, a colleague brought in a preserved bullfrog specimen that one of his students had drawn to his attention. Although it was supposed to be a male and had been ordered from the supplier to be a male, he reassured me that the frog did, in fact, have oviducts. I examined the frog, observed the testes, confirming its gender as being male, but also saw the small oviducts referenced. They were unmistakable, but I was not particularly surprised to see them. Males, I noted, were known to sometimes exhibit *vestigial* oviducts, and this frog was such an example. "Hermaphroditism is never far away," I sagaciously added with a smile.

A special challenge came one day when a student brought in the skeletal remains of something. I couldn't say for certain just what. The student said his father had dredged it up while fishing in nearby Horseshoe Lake, Illinois. He wanted to know if the remains were fossilized and, if so, what sort of an animal left the fossilized bones. I pondered the massive vertebrae, four in all, noting the four-inch-long, bony extensions that projected laterally. At each end of the specimen were shallow concavities, which I took, correctly, to be surfaces for bone-to-bone articulation. The concavity at one end was larger than at the other. I knew little about fossils and was unsure about the age of the specimen, but I did note how heavy it was—too heavy to be just bone, I thought. Laying the specimen on a laboratory tabletop, I opined that the remains could possibly be those of some sort of amphibian. The larger surface for articulation at one end might have been where a skull had once been, I reasoned, and the smaller, concave surface at the other end might have been where the smaller vertebrae of a tail had once been attached. The large, heavy projections that flared to the sides might be ribs, I thought, noting this would have given the living animal a dorsoventrally compressed body, a shape characteristic of many amphibians.

Even though I was more or less satisfied with my analysis, I had lingering doubts about whether the remains were actually fossilized.

As a result, I decided to seek a second opinion. I doubted anyone in the building would know much more than I did, but it couldn't hurt to at least ask a colleague So I decided to show the articulated remains to Othello Ulysses (Otho) Forrester, a sixty-something junior high science teacher who held court in a wing located at the back of the building. I didn't know Mr. Forrester well, but I did know he had assembled a collection of science and science-related artifacts in his barn and that this collection was referred to locally as "the museum." I also knew he charged the public 50 cents per person to view his collection. Although I'd never made it over to the museum, some of my students had been there and talked about Mr. Forrester and his stuff from time to time.

When I got to his room, Mr. Forrester was straightening up after a long day. "What can I do for you?" he asked, obviously hoping it wouldn't be much.

I assembled the bones on the teacher's desk and said, "Well, one of my students brought me this specimen, or part of a specimen, from over at Horseshoe Lake. He and his father would like to know what they've dredged up. I'm pretty sure it's some sort of amphibian."

Otho looked at me in the most puzzled and disappointed way. "Where did you think the legs attached?" he inquired. (At that point, I realized for the first time there were no indications of a pectoral girdle or pelvic girdle. I felt my countenance fall.)

I tried to save face by asking a question of my own, "It is a fossil, don't you think?"

Otho glanced at the remains again and grimaced, "No, it's not a fossil. What you have is a not-so-old part of a cow's skeleton." Picking up the remains while holding the vertebrae together, he continued, "You probably thought these lateral projections were ribs—they're not—they're transverse processes of vertebrae of the lumbar region of the back."

Removing the largest vertebra, he held it up to demonstrate, "If you cut the body of this vertebra in half, along the center of the backbone, and then remove half the vertebra and turn it on its side, the transverse process will become the bone that separates the tenderloin from the other meat of a T-bone steak!"

I was humiliated, ashamed to ask more. My good grade in comparative vertebrate anatomy now seemed undeserved. My inability to reason critically at a critical time made it a farce, a sham. Why had I not recognized that the large, lateral projections were not ribs? They did not articulate with the vertebrae, they were *part of* the vertebrae. Why had I not questioned the missing pectoral and pelvic girdles? Everything seemed so obvious now.

The next day, after class, I pulled aside the student who had initially brought me the bones. "Mr. Forrester and I did some more thinking about the bones you brought in from Horseshoe Lake," I said. "We've decided they're not fossilized and that they're probably from a cow's backbone."

The Bird Man

I didn't know Johnny Parsons as a young man. When I first met him, he was a forty-something-year-old biology professor, and I was a senior in college. I had finished my general education requirements as well as the specified courses for a major in physics. It was my last semester before graduation, and I was looking for an elective, something interesting but not too difficult. A friend had mentioned that Dr. John Parsons was a great teacher who offered a course in ornithology. I took a chance and enrolled. It was a decision that changed my life.

Ornithology is, of course, a specialized branch of biology dealing with birds. That was about all I knew when I enrolled, and to tell the truth I didn't expect to learn a whole lot more. My plan was to check out the spring warblers, take a field trip or two, and not work too hard.

The first class period provided an overview of the course, a list of recommended field-identification manuals, and a description of ideal specifications for binoculars intended for use in birding. Later classes dealt with vertebrate evolution, bird anatomy, feather terminology, song and sound production, reproductive behavior, taxonomy, and so on. Not all topics were inspirational, but by mid-term I was starting to enjoy ornithology. As advertised, Parsons was a great teacher. As graduation loomed, I found myself wishing the course could go on.

After graduation, I attended graduate school at Ohio State and later joined Bell Laboratories in Columbus, Ohio. There I met and married Mary Ann. We settled down and eventually had two boys, Charles and James. Our house was on a large lot in a wooded subdivision, a location that attracted many birds to our yard and winter-time feeder: titmice, wrens, chickadees, juncos, sparrows, nuthatches, goldfinches, cardinals, towhees, and woodpeckers of several kinds. During spring and fall, many migrants passed through, thereby adding variety and seasonal interest. As time went on, birdwatching became something that drew our family together. The boys enjoyed birds and bird lore, and their enjoyment of birds became a bond that tied them to their mother and me. As my family grew and developed, my thoughts often turned to Dr. Parsons and his vast knowledge of birds and how he had opened my eyes to a world I had not known.

Years passed before my work took me to Textron Industries in Nashville, Tennessee. Textron was a builder of airplane wings and developer of stealth technology. In fact, the B-1 bomber wing was engineered at Textron using ideas adapted from bird wing design. Since my alma mater was only thirty miles or so away, I attempted to contact Dr. Parsons. To my delight, I learned he was retired but still lived in the vicinity.

Mary Ann and I soon rekindled a long-neglected friendship with the good doctor. He came to our house for meals, and we engaged in long after-dinner conversations about many subjects: antique firearms, early Ohio and Kentucky history, the Shawnee Indian tribe, his experiences as a Lt. Colonel in charge of the U.S. Army's homing pigeons during World War II, sports, travel, and politics. More than anything else, we discussed birds. Our conversations were great, but our relationship soon progressed beyond talk. We enjoyed frequent birding trips together and became field reporters for the Tennessee Ornithological Society and assisted in its annual Christmas count.

Parsons stopped by our home often, and we learned to think of him as family. He met our grandchildren, taught them about birds, and treated them as his own. We learned about his lost loves and reasons why he'd never married. We learned of his travels to study birds in far away places. We learned of his love of hunting and the outdoors. We learned of his roots in Augusta County, Virginia, and of his early life in the mountains of Kentucky. And we learned the names of some of his friends. One friend in particular stood out: Dr. Clem Gerstenschlager, a retired professor of agriculture and education.

During their retirement years, Parsons and Gerstenschlager often spent morning hours together. They shared an interest in birds. Gerstenschlager was a builder of clever home designs for the eastern bluebird. The disappearance of wooden fence posts had led to a downturn in the number of bluebirds, and he was determined to personally assist in the revival of one of his favorite birds. He built bluebird houses by the dozen and gave them away to anyone willing to mount them properly.

Parsons often stopped by Gerstenschlager's home and accompanied him on trips to investigate reports of occasional sightings of an exotic bird of some sort. One time, they spotted a scissor-tailed flycatcher sitting on a high wire fully four hundred miles east of the area the bird normally inhabited! They monitored the state's bald eagle population and debated whether the ivory-billed woodpecker might still be extant.

Parsons and Gerstenschlager were alike in many ways: both were short, both grew up in Appalachia, both were high school valedictorians, both had potbellies, both had been professors, both loved bird life, and both admired beautiful women. Despite being alike in many ways, they were friendly but highly competitive adversaries. If one reported having sighted a pileated woodpecker, the other would report having seen two or three, that sort of thing. Although each could claim to be unique, friends and acquaintances always saw them together and thought of them as two peas from the same pod.

Johnny and Clem were partners in many adventures. For example, they often made morning birding forays to nearby sites before returning to campus and the faculty lounge for a cup of coffee. One spring morning the two ventured out to a park near an old mill site on the Stones River. Only a few people were present, and the two did not become aware of the fact that they themselves were objects of study until later. But as it turned out, a young woman who may have had a couple of drinks had noticed them and watched them from a distance. When the two started to leave, the woman intercepted them to inquire about their activities and whether they had found what they had come to see. They told her they were birdwatchers who had seen most of what they had come to see but had not seen the rose-breasted grosbeak they'd seen earlier. Apparently, the bird had migrated northward, they surmised.

"Well, would you like to see one?" the woman asked.

Perplexed but interested, the two replied almost simultaneously, "Have you seen one?"

"I can show you one," she said, and boldly peeled off her top, revealing a braless upper torso highlighted by full, rounded breasts. Seeing the faces of the flabbergasted old-timers, she laughed and said, "Now you can tell your friends you saw a rose-breasted grosbeak!"

The men returned to campus, ready to enjoy their coffee and relate their unlikely story. The story soon found its way around the coffee shop and in time entered the realm of legend.

When I enrolled in Johnny Parsons's class, I never dreamed of the significance of that single act. But looking back, it changed my life. Birding gave me pleasure beyond measure for decades thereafter. Through it, I made new friends and established special bonds with my children and grandchildren. I learned about nature and my place in it. In the end, I learned less about how to "make a living" but more about how to "make a life."

Johnny is gone now, but his influence grows larger by the day, gives immeasurable joy, and lives immortally.

In *Sweet Salvation*, the hymns quoted are from
Hymns Old & New, hymns 110 and 81, published by
R. L. Allan & Son, Ltd., Glasgow, Scotland, 1951.

www.ingramcontent.com/pod-product-compliance
Lightning Source LLC
Chambersburg PA
CBHW021926170626
46807CB00007B/2996